"Maybe You Should Consider Slowing Down,"

Danielle teased, then took a sip of wine.

"I will . . . if you'll promise to marry me," Peter replied.

Danielle barely kept from choking. "You're doing it again—saying things you don't mean, just like you did the night we met."

"I've meant every word I've ever said to you Danni," he said seriously.

"Peter, please . . . It's hard enough to believe I'm here."

"You mean I'm not your type," he said flatly.

"No, it's not that. It just seems that . . . I'm not anybody's type," she blurted out.

"Thank heaven I met you when I did," Peter said softly. "I'm a lucky man."

ANGEL MILAN

is an adventurer. Though she didn't learn to ski until she was thirty-five, she has tried almost everything else. She is not only a licensed pilot, registered X-ray technician, and former member of the Denver Classic Chorale, but is also the mother of four and grandmother of two.

Dear Reader:

SILHOUETTE DESIRE is an exciting new line of contemporary romances from Silhouette Books. During the past year, many Silhouette readers have written in telling us what other types of stories they'd like to read from Silhouette, and we've kept these comments and suggestions in mind in developing SILHOUETTE DESIRE.

DESIREs feature all of the elements you like to see in a romance, plus a more sensual, provocative story. So if you want to experience all the excitement, passion and joy of falling in love, then SILHOUETTE DESIRE is for you.

Karen Solem
Editor-in-Chief
Silhouette Books

ANGEL MILAN
Danielle's Doll

Silhouette Desire
Published by Silhouette Books New York
America's Publisher of Contemporary Romance

SILHOUETTE BOOKS, a Division of Simon & Schuster, Inc.
1230 Avenue of the Americas, New York, N.Y. 10020

ISBN: 0-671-49544-5

First Silhouette Books printing August, 1984

10 9 8 7 6 5 4 3 2 1

America's Publisher of Contemporary Romance

Printed in the U.S.A.

BC91

Books by Angel Milan

Silhouette Special Edition

Autumn Harvest #39

Silhouette Desire

Snow Spirit #34
Sonatina #64
Summerson #96
Out of Bounds #118
Danielle's Doll #153

Thank you and appreciation to Evelyn Ems,
friend and general contractor

Danielle's Doll

1

Danielle Britton heard the slam of a car door and glanced toward the street. A tall, slender man in jeans, boots and a dusty beige cowboy hat walked around the front end of a battered pickup truck and started up the brick driveway of Nathan Frost's home. From her vantage point atop a ladder on the side of the two-story house, she could see nothing of his facial features until he unexpectedly looked up.

"'Morning," he said, his friendly blue-green eyes twinkling in a parenthesis of well-established smile lines.

Danielle didn't speak but simply raised her hand in greeting so as not to encourage conversation. She was in a hurry to finish staining the wooden trim of the windowsill and get back to her office. The painter who was supposed to be completing the job had called in with the flu, and Danielle had gladly left the paperwork on her desk for a chance to get away. Still, she had to get back as soon as possible: Her biggest contract awaited her.

Through the open window Danielle heard the door-

11

bell, then two men's voices. There were heavy footsteps on the wooden stairs, and she saw the two men enter the study on the second floor. The visitor had removed his hat, and Danielle thought he looked vaguely familiar. She brushed on the last stroke of stain, picked up the can and descended the ladder. She could still hear the conversation going on above her.

"You've done yourself up pretty good here, Nathan," a man's voice said.

"I thought you'd like it, Peter," Nathan said.

"Looks kind of like a greenhouse," Peter said.

"That's what it's supposed to look like," Nathan said. "I figured if I'm going to spend half my life in this room, I'd better do something with it that makes me happy."

Danielle smiled. She had designed the addition to Nathan Frost's study, and the compliment was well appreciated. Her satisfied customers kept Britton General Contracting in business.

Nathan Frost was a writer who spent most of his waking hours in the once dark and dreary study on the south side of his home. He'd told Danielle nothing more than that he wanted plants and fish and lots of light. Danielle had taken it from there and fashioned a cantilevered addition of wood-framed glass and gleaming oak floor that expanded the room by half. Variously shaped redwood and ceramic planters with their own automatic watering system lined the glass walls, and two cylinders of thick glass reached almost to the ceiling, each one a self-contained saltwater aquarium stocked with tropical fish.

"Well, this would make me plenty happy, I'll say that," Peter continued. "I don't think I've ever seen anything quite like it . . . except maybe in a magazine."

Danielle heard more footsteps, then felt as if she were being watched as she knelt on the grass below. She continued with her work, gathering tools and covering cans without looking up.

"Britton does good work," Nathan said. "Ol' Danni can drive a nail as well as you can ride a bull, Peter."

"*Could* ride, you mean," Peter said. "I wouldn't go anywhere near a bull nowadays."

As soon as Nathan had mentioned bull-riding, Danielle knew who the visitor was, although she'd never met him. He was Peter Weston, once the star of the rodeo circuit and darling of every woman who'd ever seen him ride the wild bulls. She vaguely remembered reading about a fall he'd taken that had finally eliminated him from the competition. But New Mexico still proudly claimed him as yet another great western hero from the Land of Enchantment.

Danni adjusted the flat, billed cap she wore and began carrying her equipment to the truck backed up in the drive. She could no longer hear what the men were saying, and when she turned around, there was no one standing in the new glassed-in enclosure.

In Nathan's backyard Danni removed her gloves, took a long, cool drink from the garden hose, then started back toward the ladder.

"Hey, Danni. Come on up. I want to ask you something," Nathan called through one of the windows.

Danni loaded the ladder into the truck, then went inside and up the stairs. Peter Weston was no longer in the room. "What is it, Nathan?" she asked.

The tall, prematurely gray-haired man leaned down a bit and placed a kiss on Danni's cheek. "Thank you . . . that's first. I couldn't be happier with the results, Danni."

"I thought you'd feel that way," Danni said. She'd known Nathan for several years, and he was a close friend of her parents'.

"How's Boyd doing in the mortgage business?" Nathan asked. "Isn't he getting kind of restless sitting behind that desk of his?"

"Dad misses being out on a construction site, but he just can't do it anymore," she said.

"His back still bothers him, I know," Nathan said sympathetically. "Too bad about that accident." He gave his head a shake, then said, "I haven't seen Frances in a long time, Danni. Is she well?"

"Mother's fine. She seems to enjoy taking care of Kristy for me," Danni said.

"Who wouldn't enjoy that precious little baby girl of yours?" Nathan said with a smile.

Danni laughed. "She's a handful now, Nathan—almost four years old and into everything. You haven't seen her in a while."

"Well, I'd like to. You could bring her over to meet my niece in December. We could have a tea party and celebrate Kristy's birthday."

"I'll do that. I know she'd like to see her 'uncle' Nathan again. Talking on the phone is one thing; hugging is another."

"Danni, did you happen to see that man who was just here?" Nathan asked.

Danni nodded. "I saw him. Peter Weston, right?"

"Right. He's a longtime friend of mine and he asked me to do him a favor."

"What kind of favor, Nathan?"

"If you have the time, he'd like for you to go out to the Weston ranch this evening and talk about an addition he wants put on the main house. He was really impressed with your work."

Danni took a deep breath and let it out. "He asked for me personally?"

"Not exactly." Nathan rubbed his forehead. "He asked for the boss. He said to have someone from Britton's call him and make an appointment. I think you should handle it, Danni."

"You know what my evenings are like, Nathan. I spend them with Kristy. . . . We have so little time together." She shook her head. "Maybe I could send Sally instead."

14

"You could go after Kristy goes to bed, couldn't you?" Nathan asked.

Danielle paused, then gave in: "I guess so. Where is the Weston place?"

"East on Interstate 40, then north on the ranch road for a few miles. Living in Cedar Crest, you'd be closer than anyone else. Here, I'll draw you a map." Nathan crossed to his long oak desk and began drawing on a piece of typing paper.

Danielle couldn't help but feel that Nathan was pushing her into something she really didn't have time for. She didn't know what his reasons were, but Nathan was a good friend and she wouldn't disappoint him. If his friend wanted to see the boss, then that's who he'd see.

"Mr. Menendez is here to see you, Ms. Britton," Roberta told Danni when she came back to her office.

"Did he say what he wanted to talk to me about?" Danni asked her secretary.

"He didn't tell me anything, just said he'd wait in your office. I pulled the Valverde file for you."

"Good thinking, Roberta. Keep it in your desk for now until I find out what he wants. Where's Sally?"

"Ms. Rivers went out to the Belmonde site about an hour ago," Roberta said. "She said to tell you she's just about finished putting that bid together for the small single-family houses."

"That's great," Danni said. "How long has Mr. Menendez been waiting?"

"He just got here," Roberta answered.

"That's good. I don't like to keep people waiting. Fingers crossed?" she asked.

Roberta held up both hands, showing crossed fingers. She winked. "Good luck."

"Thanks," Danni said as she entered her mahogany-paneled office and walked to the fifty-year-old man who was just rising from the chair before her desk. "Park Menendez, how have you been?" She extended her hand to the powerfully built black-haired man. "I haven't seen you since we finished the Hanover tract." A step back and a quick glance at the firm jaw and smooth, dark complexion assured her that he looked healthy despite— or rather because of—his propensity toward hard work. "You look well."

"Thanks, Danielle. You look just fine yourself." He took his seat again as she went behind her desk and sat down. "Looks like being the boss agrees with you," he said.

"Can't complain, Park. How's Valverde coming along?"

Park tilted his head and sighed. "Do you know the developer?" he asked as Danni sat down.

"Emmitt French, isn't it? . . . We've met," she said when Park nodded.

"He's a tough cookie to work with, Danielle. You sure you want to make this bid?"

"I'm very sure. Valverde is the only mall job in town right now, and it's going to be the largest mall in the state when it's done. We can use the credit, Park. Isn't that why you bid on the prime contract?"

"You know this is the second time the bidding's been opened for the inside finishing, don't you?"

"I'm looking at it as an opportunity, Park, not as a potential problem."

"That's the way to do it," Menendez said, then leaned forward. "I've known your father for a long time, Danielle. I felt like I owed you a warning. Valverde's had some troubles."

"I appreciate your concern, Park. I've kept up with your progress and I know it's been slow for one reason or another. I'll worry about the troubles after Britton gets the bid. We can handle it."

"J. P. Humphry is throwing his hat in the ring," Park said.

"So I hear. That should make French happy," Danni said.

Menendez shrugged. "I try to stay out of Emmitt's business as much as I can," he said, reaching down beside his chair and bringing up a long roll of paper. "I thought you might need to look at this. It's a new addition that you probably haven't seen. French is hoping to get another Desert Gazer restaurant in this section."

Danni spread the blueprints across her desk and looked at the one on top. "Quite an expansion at this stage, isn't it, Park?"

"Just another of our little headaches, Danielle," Park said. He stood up. "I'll leave those prints with you for a day. You'll probably want to take a look before you revise your bid accordingly."

"I'll be out to the site tomorrow. Thanks, Park."

"Tell Boyd hello for me, will you?"

"Dad will be glad to hear from you. Take care."

Menendez turned at the doorway. "You take a little of that advice, too, Danielle," Park said then left the office.

Danielle leaned back in her chair, lifted her hands behind her head and closed her eyes. She'd been working toward a job like the one at Valverde for the three years she'd been running Britton General Contracting. If she won the contract, it would be the largest and most important one they'd had since she'd taken over the business. But that wasn't the only significant thing about it.

When her father, Boyd Britton, had been forced to retire from the construction business because of a back injury, Danielle's mother, Frances, had confided that she was actually overjoyed. Boyd had always been a workaholic, and he had left Frances pretty much to her own devices most of the time. When Danielle was young, Frances had found her fulfillment in being a wife and mother. After Danielle had left home, Frances had floundered, moving from one volunteer job to the next, trying to keep busy and feel useful.

After Boyd finally admitted that he could no longer handle the contracting business, Frances had hoped that it meant her husband would begin spending some time with her. She had plans for the two of them to do some traveling and sight-seeing. Her plans were short-lived. Boyd had gone to work just three months after the accident that had put him in the hospital. He now worked for a large lending institution that specialized in mortgages.

Danielle pulled her cap from her head and threw it on the blueprints on her desk. It made her angry every time she thought of how her mother had taken the news of Boyd's new job. She'd been devastated, and at the same time she'd congratulated him on his success—with tears in her eyes.

Getting the Valverde contract would mean extra money in Danielle's pocket, and she had special plans for it. It would pay for an around-the-world cruise for her parents. She hadn't decided what she'd do if Boyd refused to go, but day by day she was arming herself with arguments for his excuses.

Danielle looked down at the blueprints Menendez had brought to her, studied them for a moment, then rang for Roberta.

"Yes?"

"Bring the Valverde file and a gross of pencils. We've got a lot of work to do."

"Be right in."

By the end of the day Danielle had managed to revise the Valverde bid with the help of the blueprints that

Park Menendez had brought her. All that was left to do was to take one last look at the mall site and double-check her calculations against what was actually going on with the construction. Roberta had set the appointment with Peter Weston for eight thirty that evening.

"I called Penny to see if she could baby-sit tonight," Roberta said as she slipped into her sweater. "She said she'd be there at eight, all right?"

"Roberta, you're an angel." Danielle gave the small blond woman a quick hug. "I couldn't do any of this without you."

At five feet two, Roberta looked up at Danielle, who towered over her at five feet nine. Roberta's green eyes twinkled mischievously through her rimless glasses. "Sure you could," she said. "But you'd be dead in a week."

"More like twenty-four hours," Danielle said. "Jay Humphry doesn't know what he's missing by not having you in his office."

"I just thank my lucky stars that I had the good sense to quit over there when I did," Roberta said candidly.

"It's *my* lucky stars that should be congratulated, Roberta," Danielle said as she put on her denim jacket. "You have a good night now."

"After a day like today, I'll probably sleep through dinner," Roberta said. "Do you have everything you need for the Weston appointment?"

Danielle took a quick look through the briefcase that was open on Roberta's desk. "Everything," she said. "Thanks, Roberta. See you in the morning."

"Early again?" Roberta asked.

Danielle sighed. She felt badly that so much over-time had been needed since the request for proposals had come out for the Valverde job. "Just a couple more days of this, Roberta. Then maybe we can all relax."

"See you at seven," Roberta said cheerfully.

"Kristy?" Danielle called out as she entered the front door of her parent's home. "Where's my little Kristy doll?"

"In here," Frances said from the den.

Danielle hung her cap and jacket on the coatrack in the foyer and went through the door to her left. Her mother sat at a photo-strewn round table near the front windows. "Where's Kristy?" Danielle asked, sitting down across from her mother.

Frances looked up from her work. "She's next door, playing with Jean's granddaughter. Jean'll bring her back as soon as I call and tell her you're here."

"Looks like you've been busy today. What are you doing?" Danielle asked, and picked up one of the photos.

Frances put her hand on a stack of albums with black paper sheets. "The pages in these old books are starting to fall out, so I thought it would be nice to transfer the pictures to these new ones." She picked one up from the floor and handed it to her daughter.

"Mmm, these are nice," Danielle said as she opened the book. "Easy too. Just lift the plastic and put the picture right in."

"No glue, no tape. I don't know why I didn't get this kind to begin with," Frances said.

Danielle smiled. "Has Kristy been a big help to you?" she asked.

Frances smiled back. "You're expecting me to say no, but she really is helping. She's getting such a kick out of seeing your baby pictures, and she's just as careful as she can be." Frances got a faraway look in her eye. "Lots of memories here, Danni," she said, then sighed. "Mostly pleasant ones, I'm glad to say."

Danielle absently picked at the photos before her:

college graduation, Frances in her hospital guild uniform, Danielle in her wedding dress beside Lloyd Everard. . . . She stared down at the picture. That one had turned out to be the most unpleasant memory of all, she thought.

At age twenty-four Danielle had married Britton's number-one carpenter, Lloyd Everard, after knowing and working with him for a year. It had seemed like the perfect match: They shared their work, they enjoyed horseback-riding and other diversions and they both loved children and wanted a family.

Danielle had become pregnant in the second month of their marriage, and their happiness seemed complete. But the pregnancy was a difficult and complicated one. The baby was stillborn, and Danielle was informed that she would never be able to have another child.

From that moment the once happy couple had become as strangers. When Danielle needed support in her grief, Lloyd gradually withdrew from her completely. One month after the delivery, her husband moved out of the house to an apartment. Infrequently during the next month he would call and ask about her health. By the third month of their estrangement his calls stopped completely.

The last word Danielle had received from him was a letter requesting a divorce. The letter said that his desire for a family was so great and his aversion to adoption so strong that he couldn't go on being married to a barren woman. Though devastated, Danielle consented to his wishes immediately.

"Oooh . . . look at this one, Danni," Frances crooned. "Kristy was only two weeks old here." She handed the picture across the table, her eyes misty with happy memories.

"She was a beautiful baby, wasn't she, Mother?"

Frances nodded. "I had a call from Beverly just last week. Did I tell you?" Frances asked.

"What did my cousin have to say?" Danielle asked cautiously.

"You know she started college this fall?"

"Last month?" Danielle asked.

"That's right. Well, now she's married. Says her husband's handsome and well-to-do."

"You mean she was in college for only a month?" Danielle asked.

"About three weeks, actually," Frances said. "Sounds like the same old Beverly, doesn't it? If something doesn't suit her, she changes it or gets rid of it."

Danielle put the baby picture down. "I can't really complain about the way Beverly conducts her life, Mom. It's because of her impulsiveness that I have Kristy."

Frances Britton shook her head. "Pregnant at fifteen. What a disaster that could have been."

"We can't really say that for sure," Danielle said. "Beverly might have been a perfectly good mother if she'd taken the chance and kept Kristy."

"That's just the point," Frances said. "She didn't keep her. She didn't even want to see that baby when she was born. You only had to ask her once, and she was ready for the adoption papers to be drawn up that very day. Remember?"

Danielle leaned back in her chair and stretched her long legs out to the side of the table. "I remember," she said. "What a day that was. . . ."

For the first year after her heartbreaking divorce, Danielle had mourned the loss of her child and her husband. She worked harder with her father than she'd ever worked before, not only in the construction end of Britton's, but also in promoting the company. She brought in almost more business than they could handle.

By the end of the second year, she'd amassed enough money to build her own home, finance a small shopping strip in nearby Belen, New Mexico, and make a few wise real estate investments for her future. It was just after her home in Cedar Crest was finished that the thought of adopting a child began to tease her mind.

The adoption agencies hadn't given her too much hope as a single person, however, and her dream of having a baby of her own began fading after several inquiries. Then, just a week after Boyd Britton's disastrous accident, Beverly Rhodes confided in her cousin: Beverly was pregnant and thinking of having an abortion.

Danielle had promised not to tell Beverly's parents if Beverly would just give herself a week to think about her decision. It was a difficult week for both of them, but by the end of it Beverly had made up her mind. The rest was a dream come true. Beverly consented to carry the child, then allow Danielle to adopt it. Beverly's parents were kind, understanding and supportive. The papers were drawn up and Danielle's life was turned upside down— her father's retirement, a business to run, then a new baby in the house.

"I guess I'm one of the luckiest people in the world," Danielle said.

"Now, if you could just find . . ." Frances glanced up at her daughter, put down the pictures she was holding and stood up. "I'll call Jean and tell her you're here."

"Thanks," Danielle said shortly. Frances had been about to deliver the same old admonition: Danielle needed a husband.

"Bizzy and I had fun today, Mommy," Kristy said when they were finally out of the winding streets of the Four Hills residential section and headed east on the interstate. "Jill has a tea set."

"How long is Jill going to stay with her grandmother? Did she say?" Danielle asked.

"Maybe a hundred years . . . but maybe till Saturday." Kristy adjusted her doll, Bizzy, so she could see out the window. "Jill wants a Bizzy doll too. Can you make her one, Mommy?"

"I really don't have the time, Kristy. I'd like to, though."

"Maybe when you retire, like Granddaddy did?" she asked.

Danielle was always amazed at Kristy's perception of the world. Being mostly in the presence of adults had made her wise beyond her years: She would be four in December. "Making dolls would be fun to do when I retire. That's a very good idea, Kristy."

"I can help you, can't I?" Kristy asked.

"Of course you can. You already do, did you know that?"

"How?" Kristy asked.

"Sometimes you hand me things that I need, don't you?"

"You mean like a screwdriver or a nail?"

"Exactly. You're a big help."

Kristy sat a little taller and turned Bizzy so that she could look in the doll's face. "I could paint the eyes, and sew the skirt, and . . ."

"When you're a little older, you'll be able to do it all, Kristy. We'll have a lot of fun."

"We already have lots of fun," Kristy said simply.

"And we'll never stop. I promise."

Mid-September evenings on the eastern slope of Sandia Mountain were chilly as a rule, but the house that Danielle had built was a cozy place. The two-story A-frame was constructed almost entirely of fragrant cedar planks and had a deep front porch and balcony above that faced the rising sun. Front and back, there were great triangular expanses of glass with a view of the hills to the east, the Cibola National Forest to the west.

Inside, there were four fireplaces. Two tall chimneys of native stone rose from the living room and kitchen, through the upper flooring, to the two bedrooms above. Of the four hearths, the one in the kitchen got the most use.

Kristy carried a small branch from the woodpile and helped set the fire in the grate in the family-room end of the kitchen. When the kindling had been set ablaze, Danielle prepared a simple meal of ground-beef patties, potatoes baked in the microwave oven and a fresh vegetable salad. Neither of them were finicky about what they ate, but both preferred simple foods that were easy to prepare, especially since Kristy liked to help.

The child's abilities seemed to increase each day; she was already competent at making toast, washing vegetables, peeling carrots and setting the table if Danielle handed her the dishes. She was tall for her age, just as all those on Frances's side of the family were tall: Frances, her sister, Joanne, and Joanne's daughter, Beverly.

At first Danielle had worried about Kristy's height: Danielle herself had been the tallest person in her class from kindergarten through her junior year in high school. It hadn't been easy. On the brighter side, she felt she could help Kristy over the rougher spots by letting her know what to expect beforehand.

The large, friendly kitchen ran the full length of the back of the house and incorporated a family room area as well. Most evenings after dinner during the cold weather, Danielle and Kristy would sit before the fire and Kristy would play with the dollhouse and furniture that Danielle had built for her. Danielle usually kept her hands busy at night, making pieces of doll furniture.

The dollhouse was almost completely furnished with handmade fantasy-size pieces of every imaginable kind. Rather than the tiny, doll-size furniture that most regarded as playthings, the objects were in the miniature range, eight to fifteen inches high. Some of her friends were shocked that Danielle would allow Kristy to touch the exquisite pieces, but Kristy handled each one with loving care. Nothing had ever been broken.

"Uh-oh." Danielle looked at her watch. "Where has the time gone, Kristy? It's eight o'clock."

Kristy left Bizzy lying on a replica of a Louis XV chaise longue and went to where her mother was sitting. "I'll help," she said, and tried to lift the heavy wooden tool tray from Danielle's lap.

"It won't be long till you can lift that, Kristy. Here, put your fingers under the handle. I'll help you."

"Hi, folks," Penny said as she opened the back door and entered the room. "Am I on time?"

"Exactly," Danielle said as she stood. "Kristy, you have fun in your bath. I'd better be on my way."

"Roberta said you were going to the Weston ranch," Penny said. "Ah . . . this is probably silly . . . but . . ."

"What is it, Penny?" Danielle asked.

Penny dug into the pocket of her down vest and brought out a folded piece of newsprint. "I have this picture of Peter Weston. Do you think he might autograph it for me?" she asked shyly.

Danielle took the paper from her. "Won't hurt to ask."

"Is he a friend of yours, Ms. Britton?" the girl asked hopefully.

"I've never met him. I'm going out to see what he wants done to his house, that's all."

"Oh, well . . . if you don't think—"

"I'll ask, Penny. He'll probably be flattered." Danielle crossed the room to the table in the bay-windowed eating nook and picked up her briefcase. "I won't be long." She leaned down and gave Kristy a kiss. "See you later, doll."

The drive took a little longer than Danielle had expected, although the map Nathan had drawn for her proved completely accurate. The ranch house was farther north off the interstate than she thought it would be, and for several miles she was sure she was lost.

Finally a sprawling adobe structure came into view as she crested a small rise. The moon was almost full, but the tan of the exterior stucco made the building difficult to distinguish from the surrounding desert. However, several cars could easily be seen parked in front of the house, and Danielle was relieved that she could recognize the pickup truck she'd seen that morning.

Nathan hadn't told her anything about Weston ranch and Danielle was thoroughly surprised. It didn't look at all like her notion of a ranch house. Instead of a two-story wooden structure, it was a low adobe building that seemed to ramble through the clumps of bear grass and juniper and scrub oak that surrounded it. A long red-tiled porch with many columns that curved into several arches wrapped around the front and nearest side.

Danielle found her way to the front door, which was dimly illuminated by a wrought-iron–and–amber-glass light fixture. She rang the bell and waited. Voices could be heard coming from somewhere inside. She rang again. The door opened.

"It was the doorbell, all right," the dark-haired woman said, looking back over her shoulder. "Dan Britton?" she asked as she looked back at Danielle.

"Danielle," she said.

The woman's large brown eyes widened, then narrowed as she grinned. "Oh, boy," she said. "This I've got to see. Come on in." She raised an eyebrow. "I *think* Peter's been expecting you."

Danielle entered the large foyer, then was led through a wide archway straight ahead into the living room. There were several people present, all well dressed in various types of southwestern attire. A party seemed to be in progress.

"Can I get you a drink?" the woman asked.

"No, thank you," Danielle said, feeling more and more uncomfortable with every passing second.

"Peter, get on out here. There's someone here to see you," the woman called out, then to Danielle: "He just went in the kitchen for a minute."

In the next moment Peter Weston entered the room

from a doorway on the left. He wore snug-fitting, black western-style trousers, a white shirt and boots. He seemed much taller than he had that morning, when Danielle had been looking down from the ladder. His rugged presence filled the room with an excitement that Danielle hadn't anticipated, and she knew instantly why Penny had been so enthusiastic about getting his autograph.

"Who is it, Gloria?" he asked, crossing the room. "The man from Britton's?"

Gloria held her hand out toward Danielle. "I don't think you two have met," she said, a devilish grin on her face.

Peter looked at Danielle. "Hey, you're the same fellow . . ."

Danielle took off her hat, then offered her hand. "Danielle Britton," she said.

Peter stood perfectly still for several seconds, then slowly took her hand. "Well . . . I'll be damned," he said.

2

Nathan?" Peter drew the word out in an accusatory tone as he turned his head to scan the room. "Where did he go, Gloria?"

"He took off down the hall when I went to the door," Gloria said, still smiling.

Peter held on to Danielle's hand as he looked back at her. "Would you like a drink . . . something to eat?" he asked. "We're having a little party tonight." He managed a small smile, but the look on his face was one of incredulity.

"No, thank you," Danielle said. "I can come back another time, Mr. Weston. You seem pretty busy."

"No, no, not at all. I was expecting you," he said nervously. "Ah . . . that is . . . I was expecting . . ." He glanced down; his hand was still locked with hers. "Shall I show you my bedroom?" he asked, then cleared his throat. "That's where I want to build the addition," he added quickly.

There was a good-humored murmur among the people in the room. Danielle was beginning to feel as if she were on display and completely out of place. She hadn't taken the time to change her clothes, feeling that time spent with Kristy was more important than dressing to do an estimate at a remote ranch house. Her faded jeans, blue work shirt, laced brogans and cap would have been perfect on a construction site, but not in a room full of people dressed for a party.

"Yes, that would be fine," she said quietly.

As soon as they'd gone back to the foyer and turned right down the hallway, Peter began explaining his strange actions. "I saw you this morning, didn't I?" he asked first.

"Yes, at Nathan's house," she said.

"I don't know how to say this without making a complete fool of myself," he went on, "but I thought you were a young boy."

Danielle glanced at him inquisitively.

Peter stopped walking. "I didn't mean that the way it sounded," he said as Danielle turned to see why he had stopped. "Nathan didn't tell me . . ." He put his hands in his back pockets, then pulled them right out. "What I meant was . . ."

Danielle couldn't help but smile. Peter Weston was obviously uncomfortable; Nathan Frost had played another of his innocent practical jokes—on the two of them. "I think we both owe Nathan a good one, don't you?"

Peter smiled then. "You're not angry?" he asked.

"If I were, I wouldn't still be here," she said.

"Whew," he sighed. "Well, I'm really sorry, I—"

"You don't have to apologize," Danielle said. "These things happen."

Peter's eyes softened as he looked at her. "I don't believe that for a minute. . . . I must have been blind," he said quietly.

His probing gaze jarred her senses. It was as if he were looking at a beautiful and desirable woman. She'd felt neither beautiful nor desirable for years and had the idea that he might be teasing her. "Shall we continue, Mr. Weston?" She'd had enough joking for the night.

"All right," he said softly, his eyes still holding hers. He didn't move for several seconds more, then finally started walking again.

They reached the end of the long hallway and went through tall double doors. The bedroom was quite large, but even with the lights turned on, it gave Danielle the feeling of being closed in. The ceiling was high, supported by beams of dark-stained wood; the walls were a stark white, rough stucco over the two-foot-thick adobe. The floor was a beautiful wood parquet, dotted here and there with richly colored handwoven Indian rugs. A fireplace inlaid with Spanish tile dominated the wall on their right. Except for its closed-in feeling, the room was very attractive.

Peter stayed near the doorway while Danielle crossed to the middle of the room near the foot of the bed, and looked around. Since he'd seen Nathan's study that morning, Peter had been thinking about what might be done to improve his bedroom. He hadn't brought many women there; he was too busy most of the time. But he had to admit to himself that he'd been thinking about a more beautiful place to bring his infrequent visitors. It had seemed like a very nice idea.

Now, as he watched Danielle move about the room, he couldn't seem to bring any of those other women to mind. He still felt embarrassed about mistaking this lovely creature for a man, but he could think of nothing more to say to her about it. Anything that sounded like an excuse would only make things sound worse. He leaned against the wall, folded his arms across his chest and stared at her.

The bone structure of her face was exquisite, he decided; the high cheekbones, the delicate line of her square jaw, the large blue eyes—all were in perfect proportion. Her limbs were long and graceful, her body sensuously slender and supple, her movements elegant and unhurried. His eyes finally focused on her hands, the fingers long and finely formed, as she rested them on the back of one of the chairs near the fireplace. He was wishing that they were touching him instead.

"Did you have something specific in mind, Mr. Weston?" she asked.

For an instant Peter thought she'd been reading his mind, and was jolted from his flight of fancy. "No," he blurted out as he unfolded his arms and pushed away from the wall. He grinned shyly and shook his head. "Not really," he said, embarrassed all over again. Had she been a man, he might have jokingly confided his intentions about the room.

"It feels rather enclosed," she said. "Were you thinking about something along the lines of what I did for Nathan's study?"

Peter came around the end of the bed and closed the space between them. "Nothing quite that elaborate," he said. "I'm not much good with plants either. There's a beautiful view out there, though." He pointed toward the north windows. "I guess I'd just like to see more of it."

"Would you like some more time to think about this?" she asked, almost hoping he'd say yes. The look he was giving her was making her uncomfortable.

"I'd like to talk about it right now . . . if you have the time," he said. He wanted to keep her in his presence as long as he could. "We could sit right here." He took the chair opposite the one she was standing behind.

"All right," she said, and bent to pick up her briefcase. She put it on the table between the facing chairs, putting her cap in her lap as she sat down. "I can sketch a few ideas. That might help you decide." She took some blank sheets from the case, closed it and began to draw on top of it.

The room seemed to come alive at the tip of her pencil,

each version more elaborate than the preceding one. She handed them to him one by one as she finished them.

"This is it," he said, then quickly amended his statement. "I mean, something *like* this." If she thought it was exactly what he wanted—which it was—she might leave immediately.

"You'll lose some wall space with that one. Is that all right?"

He nodded toward the south wall. "That bed hasn't been moved from there since I bought this place. I'm not going to start moving furniture at this late date."

"It does seem like the perfect place for it," Danielle said, glancing sideways at the giant king-size bed. When she looked back, Peter was staring at her with a funny, questioning gaze. In the soft light his dark eyes looked more green than blue, a perfect complement to his bronze tan and sunstreaked toffee-colored hair. Except perhaps to finish the interior, Danielle hadn't been in a man's bedroom since her husband had walked out more than five years ago.

The room seemed to be closing in on her even more than it had been earlier. She brushed at a long tendril that had escaped from the wide silver barrette that held her hair in a heavy twist; she wished she hadn't removed her hat. Not that the classic little driving cap could have shielded her from the piercing eyes of the man across from her. They seemed to be penetrating her very soul.

"What changes would you like?" she asked, trying to dispel the confined feeling.

"On what?" Peter asked, the paper in his hand forgotten.

"You said the sketch looks something like what you want. Can you be a little more specific?"

"Oh, sure." He leaned forward and put the paper on the briefcase. "Maybe the archway to the porch could be a little wider?"

"All right." Danielle widened it with her pencil.

"I'd like to be able to see South Mountain."

"How's this?" Instead of slanting the porch roof down toward the outer edge, she reversed it and made it slope back toward the house. "I can drain it toward the front of the house," she said.

"I've never seen a roof slant backwards," he said.

Danielle held the paper and lifted the lid of the case. She brought out a black three-ring notebook and opened it. "I did this on the Moselles' place. The back of their house faces a mountain, and they wanted to see all of it that they could. See how it opens up the patio?"

Peter looked at the photo she was pointing to, then followed her finger to another on the same page.

"Or we could peak it, like this. That might not feel so strange to you," she said. "I could still tilt it back toward the house a little, but it wouldn't be noticeable."

Without saying anything, Peter turned to the next page, then the next. "Did you do all this work?" he asked in a soft voice.

"Britton General Contracting did it. I could hardly do all the work by myself," she answered.

Peter leaned back in his chair and folded his hands across his belt buckle. "All this is pretty hard to take in," he said. "I don't mean this in any unseemly way, but . . . well . . ." He moved forward again, his hands on his knees. "I've never met anyone quite like you, Danni Britton."

Danielle started to correct him, then remembered that Nathan had called her Danni in Peter's presence. She didn't mind her nickname; in fact, she rather liked it. "I'm just a person who works for a living," she said. "I like what I do." It almost sounded defensive.

"And you do it very well. I thought Nathan might have been putting me on about Britton until I saw his place today. And look at all this." He gestured toward the book of photos. "I just can't believe my eyes."

Danielle straightened. "Is it so hard to believe that a woman can do a good job, Mr. Weston?"

Peter hit his knee with his fist. "There I go again, trying to speak my mind and not saying what I really mean."

"Would you rather have a man do the job?" Danielle asked stiffly.

Peter exhaled with a short laugh. "Not by a long shot," he said. "You're hired. When can you start?"

Danielle took a folder from the case and pulled out some papers. "Here's the form I use to outline the job for the customer. Every item used is listed here, the price here." As she spoke she pointed to the various blanks that would be filled in. "We'll want to agree on a price before we set a start date."

"Here's a list of phone numbers," Danielle went on. "All these people are former customers who've consented to being called—if you have any questions about our work." She handed him the paper. "If you'll give me a couple hours' notice, I can arrange for you to see some of our work under construction." She opened the book of photos. "If you'd like to see some of these finished projects, I can arrange that too," she said, then started putting things away. "I'll send someone out tomorrow to do the initial estimate. Will there be someone home, Mr. Weston?"

"I won't be, but Art Dobbs is here all the time. He's my foreman. What time should he come up to the house?" Peter asked.

"Probably around ten. I'll call first," Danielle said.

"But you'll be sending someone else, right?"

"That's right. Is there some problem with that?" Danielle asked.

A slight smile crossed Peter's face. "If you were coming out, I was going to change my plans for tomorrow morning and be here myself."

Danielle didn't know what to say. Peter Weston

seemed to be flirting with her, and she wasn't sure how to react—nor could she understand why. She was glad that their business was concluded for the evening so that she could leave, but the newspaper photo that Penny had given her was still in the pocket of her jacket. If she took it out now and asked for his autograph, offering the classic explanation that it was for someone else, he might believe that she herself was interested in him. Still, she didn't want to disappoint her baby-sitter.

Danielle pulled the photo and a pen from her pocket. "I have a favor to ask," she said. "A friend of mine would like an autograph. . . . It's for Penny . . . if you wouldn't mind." She spelled the name as she handed him the paper.

Peter looked at her with a twinkle in his eye. "How about a trade? I'll sign the picture if you'll stay and help me celebrate."

"That's very kind, Mr. Weston—thank you—but I really can't."

Peter wondered what he could say to persuade her and, in an instant, discarded half a dozen ideas. He decided on the straightforward approach. "The ranch is finally paid for," he said, reaching into his own shirt pocket and withdrawing, then unfolding, a copy of the loan paper. "I'd be honored if you'd help me burn this note tonight."

Danielle could appreciate the importance of the moment for him, but she couldn't bring herself to accept his invitation. She was sure his flirting was the only way he could think of to ease his conscience. It was flattering that he thought it necessary to dispel any hurt her own feelings might have suffered because of his mistaking her for a man, but returning with him to the living room full of friends was too much to ask. His conscience would have to soothe itself.

Danielle closed the briefcase and stood up. "I appreciate your invitation, Mr. Weston. Congratulations on paying off your mortgage, but I have a very early day tomorrow. You understand."

"An early day? Is that the only reason you won't stay?" he asked as he signed his name across the bottom of the photo.

"I simply have a lot to do. I'm sure it would be a very pleasant evening, Mr. Weston," she said.

He captured her hand as she reached for the photo. "I have to tell you," he said, looking deeply into her eyes. "You've been a very pleasant surprise for me, Danni Britton."

She probably should have put an end to his solicitous flirting right then and there, she decided later as she was driving home. But it hadn't seemed right, it wouldn't have been businesslike and it certainly wouldn't have been a pleasant undertaking. Besides, she'd been happy just to escape from the situation. A confrontation would have prolonged her stay, perhaps past the limit of her patience with his attempt to make amends.

Kristy was asleep when she got home, just as Danielle had expected she would be. Penny was delighted with her autographed photo, and Danielle had to admit to her that Peter Weston was "sooo brave and sooo masculine." Penny left the house walking on a cloud of teenage happiness.

Upstairs, Danielle looked in on Kristy, gave her a soft kiss, then turned out the night-light. Kristy only wanted it on when her mother was away from home.

In her own bedroom Danielle closed the drapes in front of the expanse of glass that was the east wall, sat down on the edge of the bed and started untying her work boots. The heavy brogans were a familiar and necessary part of her attire, but she couldn't help staring at them with new eyes. Suddenly they seemed alien, an intrusion into what ought to be a feminine world.

She let one boot fall to the floor and started on the

other. At least there's no pretense about them, she thought. They're just exactly what they seem to be—and so am I. She threw the other boot to the floor. Peter Weston's flattery was just so much blarney, she told herself, just so many empty words to cover his embarrassment. An expression related to her own trade came to mind: He'd really "laid it on with a trowel."

To her dismay she found that her hands were trembling when she tried to unbutton her shirt. The "sooo masculine" image of Peter Weston would not leave her mind. She crossed to the closet to get her nightshirt before taking a shower and caught a glimpse of herself in the tall rectangular mirror near the sliding doors. The reflection held her there.

What she saw was nothing new. A tall, slender woman dressed in decidedly masculine attire. Danielle unbuckled her belt and undid her jeans, then stepped out of them. She turned one way, then the other. They were the same legs she'd had that morning, slim, firm—nothing outstanding, she decided.

Her shirt came off next and fell to the floor. In the brief cotton panties and the wisp of a white cotton bra, her conclusion was that she looked about twelve years old. Her mother had once told her, when she was sixteen, that she looked like a high-fashion model, but the compliment had been rejected out of hand. Her friends were blossoming into voluptuous young femmes fatales, while Danielle exiled herself to the wallflower seat and simply grew taller.

In college she'd had a few suitors and finally managed to get over her sensitivity about being taller than all of her women friends. She'd even begun to think of herself as somewhat attractive. When Lloyd Everard began to take an interest in her, she finally imagined herself as a desirable woman.

But losing her baby and every chance of having another, then losing her husband, had changed all that.

She was back to the place from which she'd started. No wonder I dress like I do, she thought. I dress just the way I feel, unfeminine, undesirable and definitely unavailable.

Danielle turned her back to the mirror and removed her underthings. The realization that she dressed to fit her image of herself had never entered her consciousness with such clarity—or with such disturbing force. She turned back to the mirror.

The one part of herself she'd always admired was her face. She was truthful where that was concerned: Her face was actually very beautiful, especially her large, dark blue eyes. Looking down at her bare feet, Danielle unclasped the barrette and let her long toast-brown hair fall down her back. The caress of the silky strands on her naked skin felt sensuous and made her tremble involuntarily. She looked up and, almost hopefully, back into the mirror, then shook her head. There was nothing there that could possibly deserve Peter Weston's compliments or his interest—or any other man's, for that matter.

Danielle was at her desk a half hour before Roberta arrived. The completed Belmonde proposal for the interior finishing on the tract of small houses had been left on her desk by her assistant, Sally Rivers. After one complete reading Danielle had to start all over again. Nothing she'd read had made any sense. Her mind kept straying from the figures before her to the man who owned Weston ranch.

Penny's description of him kept entering her mind. "He's just the most manly kind of man I've ever seen. You know, rugged and strong," she'd crooned the night before. "He's just so . . . so . . . fine, isn't he?"

With seventeen-year-old Penny standing in front of her, Danielle had readily agreed that Peter Weston was indeed a "babe," the high school term for a good-looking male. But she agreed privately, too—later, while she was tossing and turning in her bed last night, and now, while seated at her desk, trying unsuccessfully to concentrate.

Peter Weston was the classic cowboy. He was tall, lean and strong, with wide shoulders and a narrow waist and hips. His thick, light-brown hair had a slight wave, so that the short cut feathered back from a brazenly angular and masculine face. Danielle had never seen him at work when he had been riding the wild bulls in the rodeo, but she'd seen him in a television commercial for some brand of beer—she couldn't remember which one. He'd also done a magazine advertisement for the same product.

That had been several years ago, but he still had that same rugged and flamboyant sensuality about him. Yet, he had a sensitive shyness about him too. One might expect him to say "Yes ma'am" or "Pardon me, ma'am" at any moment. Still, for all his reserve, he was a masculine force to be reckoned with. When he'd first walked into the living room the previous evening, it was as if the room had taken on a new and vibrant kind of energy.

Danielle put the papers down, stood up and walked away from her desk. She folded her arms at her waist and paced the length of her office and back. The movement seemed to help slightly, so she continued her pacing until she heard a quiet knock on her door and Sally Rivers walked in.

"How is it?" Sally asked immediately.

"How's what?"

"The bid for the Belmonde tract," Sally said. "Didn't you find it on your desk this morning? I'm sure I . . ." She crossed to the desk. "Here it is. Haven't you had a chance to look at it?"

"Yes . . . yes, I did look at it," Danielle said. "I'd like to go over it again before you submit it."

Sally gave her a questioning look. "Do you feel all right, Danni?" she asked.

"I'm fine, Sal. I had a late night, that's all."

"A date?" There was a touch of hope in her voice.

"No"—Danielle shook her head slowly—"a business appointment. I'm glad you came in; I want you to do an estimate on an addition today."

"What time?" Sally asked.

"He said it didn't make any difference. I told him ten, but there'll be someone there all day."

"Where?"

"Where what?"

"Danielle, are you sure you're all right? Nothing's wrong? You seem preoccupied."

Danielle frowned. "I said I was fine."

Sally raised a dark eyebrow. "In that case, why don't you tell me where it is I'm supposed to be at ten this morning."

Danielle ran her fingers over her forehead and closed her eyes for a second. "I'm sorry, Sal, I thought I had. The Weston ranch. . . . I'll draw you a map."

"Peter Weston's place?" Sally asked excitedly.

"That's it," Danielle said.

"No need for a map. I know right where it is. I was there once, at a party." Sally gave her a curious look. "Is that where you were last night?" she asked.

"He's a friend of Nathan Frost's. Nathan recommended us to him."

"Recommended us . . . or you, Danni?" Sally held up a hand. "Don't tell me why you didn't send someone else." A mischievous grin brightened her dark brown eyes. "If there was ever a more delicious eligible bachelor, I'd like to know who it is. Congratulations on your decision to go yourself."

"He asked for the boss," Danielle said defensively. "He didn't even know who that was. Sally, he saw me up on a ladder at Nathan's yesterday and thought I was a man."

"A man!" Sally's eyes widened. "He must be getting blind in his old age. How old is he now, thirty-five, -six?"

"I wouldn't have the foggiest idea," Danielle said quietly.

"But you'd like to know, wouldn't you?"

"It's hardly important how old the man is. He simply wants an addition to his bedroom. I'll show you the sketches I made."

"You were in his bedroom?" Sally asked, the impish grin returning.

"Sal, would you stop with the innuendos? Our meeting was strictly business." Her words sounded too harsh for the situation. She smiled to make up for it. "That is, as soon as he got through apologizing for mistaking me for a young boy, it was strictly business," she added, unable to keep from laughing.

"That must have been something." Sally started to laugh too. "Oh, I wish I'd been there to see his face when he realized his mistake. Tell me what happened, Danni."

It was a relief to laugh about it. The story, retold, really was funny.

". . . So he just kept up the flirting to ease his conscience till I walked out the door," Danielle finished.

A serious look crossed Sally's round face. "Why do you insist that his compliments weren't for real, Danni?"

"Come on, Sal. I wasn't born yesterday. Didn't I describe Gloria?"

"You described her well enough. So what?"

Danielle didn't like the turn of the conversation. Sally was insisting on a self-examination that was at least unpleasant if not downright frightening. She stepped behind her desk. "Let's go over the Belmonde bid, then take a look at these sketches so you'll know what you're doing when you get out to the Weston place, okay?"

Sally paused for a moment, then moved to the desk. "All right," she said softly.

A few minutes after Sally left the office, Roberta came in with the mail.

"Here are Sally's figures on Belmonde," Danielle told

Roberta. "Just fill in the forms they sent and we'll be ready to submit."

"How did it go last night?" Roberta asked.

"Routine," Danielle said.

"That's not what I heard," Roberta teased.

"Sally?" Danielle asked, and Roberta nodded. "She has a vivid imagination. Don't believe a word of what she told you."

"There's nothing wrong with a little romance in your life," Roberta said happily.

"There is if it's imaginary," Danielle countered.

"From what I hear, Peter Weston is a far cry from imaginary," Roberta said.

Danielle was staring down at a letter she held in her hand. "I suppose," she said almost inaudibly.

"What is it?" Roberta asked. "Is something wrong?"

"No," Danielle said slowly, turning the letter facedown on the desk. "There's nothing wrong. I guess I'm just a little anxious about the Valverde job," she lied.

"I'll go get this Belmonde thing put together," Roberta said, a worried look on her face. "Anything else before I start?"

Danielle shook her head. "Nothing I can think of right now," she said. Roberta left the room. As soon as Danielle was alone, she tore into the letter. It was from her cousin Beverly.

Danielle,

As Aunt Frances probably already told you, I'm married now. Gilbert is very well to do, and I'm finally happy with my life . . . except for one thing. I want Kristy back. I want her to be part of my family, now that I have one.

This may be hard for you to understand, but I'm ready to do anything that I have to to get Kristy back. It isn't right for her to be brought up by a woman who goes around dressed like a man and working at a man's job. I'll go to court if I have to.

That's all for right now. I'm sure this can be worked out peacefully and without hard feelings.

Beverly

Danielle felt sick to her stomach. She crushed the letter as her hand tightened into a fist. She stood and began to pace again, trying to clear her mind. Her actions had to be rational and right, she thought as she moved across the room.

Her cousin Beverly had always been an impulsive sort, and her rash behavior had gotten her into a lot of trouble on several occasions. This impetuous decision to gain custody of her daughter was not unpredictable by any means, but it was more frightening to Danielle than anything Beverly had ever tried.

Though she was twelve years older than Beverly, Danielle had always been her confidante of sorts. Beverly would tell Danielle about her latest escapade days before Beverly's parents inevitably found out about it. She'd managed to survive numerous speeding tickets, two minor accidents, a cheating scandal in her high school and, of course, a teenage pregnancy. Much of her success was due to Danielle's intervention and sound advice.

"Damn you, Beverly," Danielle whispered under her breath. "Why can't you just leave us alone?" She pressed the intercom button. "Get me Ernie Tadlock on the phone, Roberta. Thanks."

In a few short minutes Ernest Tadlock, Danielle's attorney, had heard the letter and evaluated the circumstances. In his opinion Beverly wouldn't have a chance of getting custody of Kristy, in court or out. "I don't think you have a thing to worry about, Danni," he said. "She obviously hasn't read the custody agreement she signed."

"I get the idea from her letter that she wants me to simply turn Kristy over to her," Danielle said.

"I'm correct in thinking that you don't have any intention of doing such a thing, am I not?" Ernie asked.

"You're absolutely right, Ernie."

"Just avoid her, Danielle. If she contacts you, tell her to have her lawyer call me. We'll get this thing straightened out in no time."

"Thanks, Ernie."

"You're always welcome, Danni. And say hello to Boyd for me."

"Will do."

But she didn't. Danielle couldn't bring herself to say anything to her father about Beverly's letter or her conversation with Ernie. By the time she'd arrived in his office to go over the Valverde bid with him, she had already decided not to tell him any of it. Not that she wasn't in the habit of confiding in him; she was. But he would certainly tell her mother, Frances, and it wouldn't be fair to upset her unnecessarily. She was already too unhappy with her own set of circumstances.

Boyd Britton gave the Valverde bid a thorough going-over and pronounced it flawless. "You're really something, Danielle," he said. "And I'm not just saying that because you're my daughter. You really know what you're doing."

"That's the nicest compliment I've had in ages, Dad."

"Now, that's something I wouldn't bet on," Boyd said, and winked at her.

Danielle gathered her papers together and started putting them in her case.

"Anything else you wanted to talk about, Danni?" Boyd asked.

"No, nothing I can think of, Dad."

"You seem a little distracted," he said offhandedly.

"Just worried about Valverde, I guess."

"That's the best bid you've ever done. Why are you worried?"

"Jay Humphry is bidding against us," she said.

"That old toad?" Boyd snorted. "He can't do better than this." He pointed to the papers she was putting in her briefcase.

"I don't think he can, either, but you know Jay."

"And I wish I didn't," Boyd said disgustedly.

"I think Park Menendez feels the same way," Danielle said.

"I know he does," Boyd said. "If you don't get this bid, there's something fishy going on. You can bet on it."

"Well, say a little prayer. It goes in tomorrow." Danielle walked over to the door.

"Let's throw a big party to celebrate," Boyd said. "The whole company . . . and you can bring your latest beau."

Danielle started to say she didn't have one but decided to let it alone. She didn't think her father had the least idea of her isolated existence, and she certainly didn't want to go into it now. She opened the door. "I'll call you as soon as I know something," she said as she backed out of the room.

"Well, I'll be," a male voice said.

Danielle jerked her head around. The voice was familiar.

"What a lucky coincidence," Peter Weston said.

3

_____

Danielle drew a breath. "Hello, Mr. Weston."

Peter offered his hand immediately. "It's good to see you again so soon," he said, shaking her hand and smiling. "Your secretary called this morning. Art'll be waiting at the house for your man to arrive."

Danielle suppressed a smile. She wondered if Art Dobbs would be as surprised to find out that Sal Rivers was a woman as Peter had been when Danni Britton turned out not to be a man. She withdrew her hand from his. "Thank you, Mr. Weston. That'll make everything a lot easier for us."

Peter clenched his fists and glanced toward the secretary's desk. "This borrowing money makes me nervous," he said. "How about you?"

"The construction business exists on borrowed money, Mr. Weston." That sounded a little pompous, she thought. "But I can sympathize," she continued. "I've had to borrow for myself too."

Peter shrugged. "You know what I mean, then." He

glanced at the secretary again. "Say, do you have time for a cup of coffee? I don't know how much longer I'm going to have to wait, but maybe I could find out."

Danielle looked at her watch. "I'm a little behind schedule already. I really need to be going."

"Oh, that's too bad. I was thinking—"

"Mr. Weston? Mr. Britton will see you now," the secretary said.

A surprised look crossed Peter's face. "Britton?" he asked the secretary, then looked at Danielle before he got an answer. He pointed his finger toward Boyd's office door, then to Danielle, an eyebrow raised in question.

Danielle nodded.

"Well, I'll be . . ." he said softly. It took him a moment to gather his thoughts. "Have a good day, Mrs. Britton." It sounded so trite, but it was all he could think of.

"Good luck, Mr. Weston," Danielle said without correcting his second mistake about her identity, then left the office.

Peter hesitated for a moment before entering Boyd Britton's office. He wasn't prepared to meet Danni's husband, especially after the way he'd acted the night before. He'd been so taken with her that the possibility that she was married hadn't even entered his mind. Neither time they'd met had he made it a point to see if she were wearing a wedding ring.

What if she'd told her husband about his behavior toward her? he wondered. Had they gotten a good laugh at his expense? What if Britton was, at that very moment, predisposed to refusing Weston a loan? He turned to the secretary.

"You did say Mr. Britton, didn't you?" he asked. When she nodded, he went on. "Do you suppose there's any way I could see some other loan officer?"

"I'm afraid not, Mr. Weston." She looked through her schedule book. "I could get you in to see someone else next week. Is something wrong?" she asked.

Peter clenched his fists again. He'd faced tougher confrontations than this one, he decided. "No, everything's just fine. No problem." He crossed to the door, put his hand on the knob, then took a deep breath. "Thanks," he said back over his shoulder as he stepped inside.

"Ah, Mr. Weston. I've always wanted to meet Peter Weston face-to-face," Boyd said as he came around his desk to shake hands.

Peter couldn't find his voice for a moment. He cleared his throat instead as he reached for the hand offered to him. The man standing in front of him was probably sixty years old. "Glad to meet you, Mr. Britton," he managed finally.

"So . . . have a seat," Boyd said. "What can I do for you today?"

Peter sat down; his hands began to absently rub the top of his denim-clad thighs as Boyd moved behind his desk.

"Frances is going to be so jealous that I got to meet you and she didn't," Boyd said as he sat down. "She's always been a rodeo fan."

"Frances?" Peter questioned.

"My wife," Boyd said, and reached for one of the framed pictures on his desk.

When he turned it around, Peter saw a tall, slender woman of about fifty. She was almost as beautiful as Danni Britton. Peter leaned forward, smiling now. "So your wife's a rodeo fan?" he said. "That's very good to hear, Mr. Britton."

"Call me Boyd." He turned the picture back around to face him.

Peter felt a wonderful release of tension. When he'd leaned forward, he'd also seen a graduation picture—Danni's. He was ready to get down to business. "Well, Mr. Britton . . . Boyd . . ." he began.

In half an hour Peter had outlined his entire idea to

Boyd Britton. Over the years, he'd spent much of his spare time, both at home and on the road, hand-tooling leather goods, saddles, bridles, chaps, belts. He'd always done them on a piecemeal basis, either as he felt like it or when someone asked him to do something specific. Their mutual friend, Nathan Frost, had persuaded Peter that he should begin retailing the loftful of items he'd accumulated.

Boyd was surprised to learn that Peter Weston also ran a camp for children, Wild Weston's Rancheros. He'd set aside a portion of his ranch for youngsters who wanted to learn all about horses and horsemanship. At the same time he'd sold his cattle and started devoting all his time to teaching the kids and breeding and training horses.

"So you want to mortgage the ranch again and lease space in Valverde?" Boyd said, rubbing his chin thoughtfully.

"That's right. Doesn't sound like much, but from what I've been told, it can run into a lot of money," Peter said.

"That's right," Boyd said. "The first tenant in a new mall pays a heavy price just for being first. He foots the bill for everything—heating ducts, wiring, all your fixtures, lights, carpeting, you name it." He leaned forward. "Of course, you can pass that cost on if you decide to leave."

"So where do we start?" Peter asked.

Boyd folded his hands on his desk. "You're sure this is what you want to do, are you, Pete?" he asked, then went on. "You're putting a lot on the line. The mall will give you a high-traffic location and a lot of visibility, but you'll have to be prepared to cover both the note and the lease payments on your own if your loan money runs out before you're on your feet and the profits start coming in."

"I've talked with my foreman, Art Dobbs, about it. Our mares dropped some fine foals last spring. Maybe you've heard of one of our stallions, Brazos."

"Kentucky Derby?" Boyd asked.

"You name it, he's won it," Peter said proudly. "As they say, if the weather holds and the creek don't rise, we should be pretty healthy by the time Valverde is ready to open."

"Well, then, I'll see to the paperwork as soon as you get together with Emmitt French. You haven't talked to him yet, have you?"

"Nope. You're the first stop. I didn't want to get my hopes up just to find out I couldn't get the money."

Boyd stood up. "I think the loan committee will like what they see here," Boyd said, his finger tapping the papers Peter had brought in.

"Thanks, Mr. Britton . . . Boyd. Thanks a lot."

Peter didn't bother with the elevator. He fairly flew down the six flights of stairs to the main floor, then out into the parking lot. That day was one of the happiest times in his life, he decided as he backed the truck out of its parking place and headed toward the southeast part of Albuquerque.

By the time he reached the Valverde construction site, he'd realized that ninety-nine percent of his happiness was due to the fact that Boyd Britton was Danni's father and not her husband. He had to face the fact that she might be married to someone else, but if she was, she hadn't taken his name. Things were looking better and better, he thought as he got out of the truck and started for the foreman's trailer.

Getting permission to have a look around was no problem. The foreman turned out to be another rodeo fan who was overjoyed to meet the well-known Peter Weston. Peter traded his cowboy hat for a bright yellow hard hat and was on his way toward the vast steel and concrete shell of Valverde in less than five minutes.

Once inside, he had no idea what he thought he'd come to see. It was impossible to tell what the place was going to look like when it was finished. There'd been an artist's concept of Valverde in the newspaper, but only the exterior had been rendered. Peter wandered around for a while, greeting workers, admiring their work and asking questions.

Peter took an interest in the difficult labor of one of the ironworkers, and the man finally pointed out a section of the mall that was a recent addition where the basic structure was still being put into place. Peter thanked him and walked almost the full length of the cavernous building to take a look. To his complete surprise Danni Britton was standing right in the center of what seemed to be the entrance of the new portion.

He stopped walking and watched her for a few moments. There was a thick stack of blueprints unrolled and laid out on two sawhorses in front of her. Danni, another woman and an older man were talking, pointing here and there, then referring to the blueprint on top. When Danni spoke, the other two seemed to listen carefully and respectfully. Inexplicably, Peter felt proud just to know such a woman. He wanted to know her even better, he thought as he started toward them—and he vowed that he would.

She looked so relaxed and efficient in this strange setting, he mused as he closed the distance between them. The yellow hard hat seemed to make her all the more beautiful somehow, contrasted as it was by the fine wisps of hair that framed her face and curled at the back of her graceful neck. Peter had never been more intrigued by a woman.

As he was about to approach them Danielle turned and started walking away. "Hello there," he said, to get her attention.

Danielle looked back and stopped. "Mr. Weston," she said, but couldn't think of another thing to say.

"We seem to be running into each other all over the place," he said casually as he came up beside her.

"If I didn't know better, I'd think you were following me," she said with a forced smile.

"Would you object if I am?" he asked as she started walking again.

"I guess that depends on what you expected to accomplish by it," she said.

Her abruptness gave him a moment's pause. "I'm not following you," he said finally.

"I'm glad to hear that, Mr. Weston."

Danielle stopped again and watched while a girder was lifted into place by a large crane. When it had been precisely guided into position, she turned. "Why are you here, Mr. Weston?" she asked.

"I just came out to have a look around. I'm going to be leasing space here at Valverde," he said. She frowned as if she didn't believe him, so he told her about Nathan's suggestion and his plans because of it.

". . . But when I got here," he finished, "I realized I didn't have the slightest notion what I was looking for. I guess I expected everything to be neatly arranged so I could get an idea about what I'd be leasing."

In spite of herself, Danielle was impressed. For all Peter Weston's macho appearance and press in the same mode, he was a truly modest man. "It *is* difficult to imagine what's going to happen inside something this large, isn't it?" she said, and felt good about putting him a little more at ease.

"It's kind of like a mare in foal: You don't know what you'll get until you've got it," he said.

"I imagine it is," Danielle said. "I'll be glad to show you around if you have time."

Peter was delighted with his good fortune. "I've got all the time in the world," he said. They returned to the other man and woman.

"Park Menendez, this is Peter Weston," she said, and the two men shook hands. "Sally, I think you already know Mr. Weston."

"We met once." She shook his hand. "You probably don't remember me; I came to a party at your ranch with John O'Brian."

Peter's eyes lit with recognition. "Of course. You wore a bright red dress."

"The only dress at the party," Sally said to Danielle, then laughed. "John didn't tell me we'd be cooking out on a campfire."

"Sounds like John," Peter said. "How is he? I haven't heard from him since he left for Kansas."

"He's just fine. I get a letter once in a while. I told Art Dobbs hello for him this morning."

"You told Art . . . ?" Peter glanced at Danielle and she nodded. "Oh, boy," he said, and adjusted his hard hat.

Sally grinned and nodded too. "He was waiting for *Mister* Rivers," she said.

"I'm bound to make a fool of myself," Peter said, smiling good-naturedly. He looked around. "But that may be the least of my problems."

"Mr. Weston's going into the retail business," Danielle explained, then told them what he wanted to do at Valverde.

"I think you've picked the best spot in town," Park said.

"Now, if I could only pick the best one in here," Peter said.

"We'll have a look around," Danielle said. "I'll be back in a few minutes, Sally."

To Peter, who'd never thought about such things to any great degree, the tour was fascinating. As when Danielle had begun sketching changes to his bedroom, the gigantic shell seemed to come to life for him as she described it.

There would be two levels on the eastern end, three on the western end. No fewer than twelve entrances to the central common were planned, and six major department stores would occupy the six corners of the modified

T shape. Peter watched her as with graceful movements of her hands and arms she described the garden that would fall in tiers from the third story on the west to the ground floor on the east.

"Over that, there'll be a hanging garden; also, that will meet the other one about there." She pointed toward the ceiling about two thirds down the center.

"You seem to know an awful lot about this place," Peter said. "Is that because you're helping to build it?"

Danielle shook her head. "Not yet. We're just hoping that we will."

"What does that mean?" he asked.

She outlined the procedure for bidding on a job such as this one. ". . . So you see, we're still in the 'crossed-fingers' stage," she finished.

Peter was intrigued. "You mean you might be the very person who finishes my store?" he asked.

"That's a possibility," she said, smiling.

"I'm going downtown to see this fellow French today," he said enthusiastically. "I wasn't exactly excited about Nathan's idea until just now." It would be almost like having Danni Britton with him all the time, he thought, her work in his home and at his place of business too. The feeling of closeness pleased him.

"The leasing was opened up even before they broke ground, so your choices may be limited," Danielle told him. "Being near one of the outside entrances is a plus in most cases."

"I'll remember that." Peter stopped near the entrance of an alcove. "What's going into that new part you were looking at?" he asked, and pointed back with his thumb.

"The Desert Gazer, for one thing," Danielle said.

"You mean that new restaurant? The same one that just opened up on the mountain?"

"That's the one," Danielle said.

"I haven't tried it yet, have you?" Peter asked.

Danielle could feel an invitation coming and was at a

loss as to how she could avoid it. "No, I haven't," she said, then turned and pointed toward the far wall. "The main parking lot will be on the north side. If you can get your space near the center entrance, or directly across the common from it, you'll have an ideal spot for your business," she said.

Peter put a hand on her waist. "I really appreciate all the help you're giving me," he said as he eased closer to her. "I realize now how busy you are."

She looked up and back at him. "No trouble," she said, and took a step away from him. Unfortunately it also took her farther into the alcove.

Peter pursued her.

Danielle felt the warmth of his presence near her again. "Actually," she said, "I admire you for trying such a risky business as retailing—especially in a place as expensive as Valverde."

"That's very nice of you to say, Danni."

"Did you consider another location?" she asked, trying to keep the conversation businesslike. Her heartbeat seemed to be doing funny things inside her chest.

"It's always been hard for me to think small," he said, moving to face her.

Danielle could appreciate his philosophy. She'd been working toward making Britton's the biggest and the best for years. "I guess this is the place to start, then," she said quietly.

Peter put a hand on the concrete wall behind her. "My thoughts exactly," he said under his breath. "May we start with a dinner date?"

He was leaning toward her, his eyes searching hers for an answer to his question. She could simply say no and be done with it, but she really didn't want to. A dinner date might be just the thing to get everyone off her back about her lack of a social life. If Frances and Sally thought she was seeing Peter Weston, they might give her some peace. Still, she herself felt some resistance to the idea.

"I'm going to be pretty busy for the next few days," she said.

"I can wait," he said.

"I'll have to look at my schedule."

"Our plans may fit together perfectly," he said. "I have to go down to San Antonio to look at a horse I might want to buy."

Danielle saw a way to get the conversation away from the two of them. "You buy horses?" she asked.

"And breed them, and train them, and sell them."

His voice was low and vibrant, threading its way through her mind and her body, provoking a shiver of anticipation. "That sounds interesting," she managed.

"I'll have to show you around the ranch sometime . . . soon," he said. "Do you like horses?"

"Yes, very much," she answered.

"Somehow I knew you would," he said softly. He touched her chin, then ran his finger back along her jaw. "You're a beautiful combination of talents and interests, Danni Britton."

"Mr. Weston . . ."

"Peter," he corrected.

"Peter, I should . . ." His hand passed her ear, then lifted the hat from her head. His face was so close that she could barely focus on it. She wanted to dart to the side and run away—her pulse was racing the way her legs should have been—but she was trapped. A step backward put her against the solid wall behind her as his lips descended. "Peter . . ." she whispered as their mouths touched.

Danielle had not felt the touch of a man for so long that she couldn't remember exactly how long it had been. What she expected and what was actually happening were two completely different things. Her senses were alert for aggression, for the intrusive trespassing she would have imagined, but Peter's kiss was tender, even tentative.

She felt herself reeling, the pressure of his firm lips undemanding yet persuasive. Her eyes closed and his touch became the center of her consciousness. The clean, outdoorsy fragrance of his skin excited her; the slight roughness of his chin sensitized her own.

Of their own volition her hands rose to his waist and lightly rested there. She could perceive no threat, but the gentle touch of his lips assaulted her senses. In the cool October air she could feel the heat of July invading her body, every vein pulsing with a strange warmth that excited and frightened her.

She was so lost in the pure pleasure of the moment she barely heard the clatter as her hat dropped from his hand and hit the floor. Then his arms were about her and a moment of fear stabbed through her. This shouldn't be happening, she told herself, not here, not now. But it was happening, and she was enjoying it.

Hard hands were at her back, pressing her forward gently. Danielle could feel him trembling slightly. Then, as quickly as it had come, the trembling was gone. It was as if he were reigning in his emotions, working to control them. His arms loosened slightly, giving her the feeling of being free but at the same time capturing her more surely than if he'd held her tightly.

"Peter Weston?" The question was voiced by a woman some distance away from them.

Danielle immediately stiffened. Sally obviously couldn't see her with Peter standing in the way. Her embarrassment was complete when Peter didn't give any inclination of moving away. His lips left hers, but he stayed where he was.

"Yes," he said, his eyes still holding Danielle's in their steady gaze.

Danielle gave a little push against him as she heard Sally's footsteps, then Sally was in a position where she could see that Peter Weston was not alone.

Sally was nonplussed. "Ah, there you are, Danielle. I

just wanted to tell you I'm headed back to the office. I think Emmitt has one more question to ask you before you leave."

Peter straightened and politely took a step back so that the two women could talk. He heard Danni ask what Emmitt wanted to know, but that was all he heard. His own thoughts were intruding on the words that were being spoken, and his thoughts astonished him.

Her career and dress notwithstanding, Danielle Britton was the most feminine woman he'd ever met. He was so used to being ardently pursued, he couldn't understand exactly what was happening to him, but he'd most definitely been caught—and he, most definitely, was not complaining.

There'd been no womanly trap set for his attentions. There'd been no coaxing or cajoling or flattery. Her elusiveness fascinated him as no amount of chasing could have. She lived every day in a man's world, but she managed to retain the ultrafeminine presence of a gentle-woman.

He could still feel the soft pressure of her lips on his, and he wanted to imagine that she'd responded much more than she actually had. The light touch of her hands on his waist had been as exciting as the most amorous kiss he'd ever received.

". . . So now Park has his blueprints," Sally was saying as she bent down, then straightened. "And you have your hat." She handed it to Danielle with a smile.

"Thanks," Danielle said, deciding not to risk an explanation of why her hat was on the ground instead of on her head. "I'll be right behind you."

"No hurry," Sally said. "There are other things as important as work."

"It was a pleasure to meet you again, Miss Rivers," Peter said as she turned toward him.

"Call me Sally," she said. "A friend of Danni's is a friend of mine."

Danielle wanted to follow Sally out of the place, but instead she stood where she was and watched her assistant go.

Peter stepped closer and took her hat out of her hand. "You still haven't told me whether you'll have dinner with me," Peter said.

"Yes . . . I will," she said.

"I'll be back from Texas in ten days, maybe sooner."

"I'll check with Roberta," she said.

"I don't care when you're free. That's the day I'll be back, all right?"

"You won't have to cut your trip short on my account," she said.

"But I want to."

"I wouldn't want you to," she said. "I don't want you to get the idea that—"

"—that you could become very important to me?" he asked.

"Peter, I'm really not in a position to . . . to . . ." She took a breath. ". . . encourage you," she finished.

"I'm not sure I know what that means, Danni," he said.

"We're going out to dinner. Let's just leave it at that, okay?"

"For right now it's enough," he said, and took her hand. "I won't rush you into anything. I promise." He looked down at the strong, long-fingered hand he held. "You're a beautiful woman, Danielle Britton. I treasure the fact that I know you."

Coming from the rough-and-tumble cowboy, his tender words seemed inconsistent with his image and his reputation, but Danielle was touched by them. "That's very nice," she said softly. "Thank you."

Peter kissed the back of her hand, something he'd never done to a woman before. It seemed totally appropriate for this woman, though illogical in their present surroundings. He could envision her in the grandest ballroom, dressed in a gown of ruffled silk, her hair falling in soft curls over her bare shoulders.

He released her hand and dug into his pocket. "I want you to take my key," he said. "That way you can start on the house anytime you want to while I'm gone."

Danielle frowned. "That's not our policy," she said.

"Take it." He pressed the key into her hand.

"We haven't come to any kind of an agreement on price or—"

"Anything you do will please me," he said.

"But—"

"You did it for Nathan. I know what he asked for and I saw what he got. I could hardly wish for more."

"I'll at least want you to know what figures Sally came up with this morning," she said.

"Fair enough. I'm going to call you tonight," he said. "Maybe you'll have checked your schedule by then and we can talk about this some more."

"All right," she said hesitantly. "I'm in the phone book."

"I already know your number." He recited it for her, then told her: "You gave me your card last night."

"You have a very good memory."

"Only about very important things."

A movement to the left caught her eye. "There's Park. I really have to go."

"I'll call," he said.

Danielle's business with Park Menendez took only moments, then she was on her way back to the office. Thinking about what had just happened, she was so totally confused by Peter Weston's actions that she missed her freeway exit and had to backtrack through several blocks of heavy traffic. The many delays at stoplights gave her too much time to ponder the situation.

The fact that Peter had come in to see her father about

borrowing money was very disturbing. On the face of it their meetings had seemed completely coincidental, until she analyzed them. The first might have been a practical joke initiated by Nathan, or it might have been a private conspiracy. Peter had told her that the idea of his going into business had been Nathan's. Logically, Nathan would have to know about Peter's need for money to finance the venture.

She didn't want to think that Nathan would try to ease Peter's risky path by lifting Boyd Britton's burden—his only daughter's companionless existence. That would be risky business in and of itself. How could Nathan know beforehand that she and Peter would even be able to stand one another?

Perhaps the conspiracy was between the two of them, Peter and Nathan, and not a private one at all, she thought, stopping at yet another red light. The idea made her shudder with revulsion, and she prayed that it wasn't true. The thought of both of them knowing her father's concern for her solitary life and using his particular anxiety for their own selfish purposes tormented her mind.

Their meeting at the Valverde site was the most confusing of all. Had her father casually mentioned the fact that she'd be there? Perhaps Peter had questioned Boyd about his daughter's work and her goals. Could he have deduced where she'd be at that moment in time? she wondered. Or was he telling the truth about being there just to inspect the location of his new business venture?

She realized as she pulled into the intersection that she hadn't given the slightest consideration to the possibility that Peter Weston might really be interested in her simply for herself. He'd actually behaved as if he found her an attractive woman, he'd told her she was beautiful, he'd said he "treasured" knowing her.

She glanced into the rearview mirror. Same face, she

thought, then looked down at her long denim-clad legs and heavy boots. Same Danielle. High Hat, they'd called her in grade school. "How's the weather up there?" they'd teased her.

She remembered looking up into Peter's eyes. It had felt good to have him towering over her, holding her as if she were fragile and precious. She didn't remember feeling that way with Lloyd, maybe because they'd been almost exactly the same height. Her train of thought was ridiculous, she decided as she turned into the office parking lot. She and Peter would have dinner together and that would be the end of it. In fact, he probably wouldn't even call her that night.

"I'll get it, Mommy," Kristy said when the phone rang at about seven thirty. "Britton residence," she said proudly in her most grown-up voice. "My name's Kristy Britton. What's yours?" Silence. "Mommy, it's Peter Weston on the phone."

Danielle's breath caught in her throat. In the course of the rest of her busy day, she'd completely forgotten about Peter's promise to call her. She took the phone from her daughter.

"Hello. This is Danielle."

"I thought I had the wrong number there for a minute," Peter said.

"No," she said.

"Nathan told me you had a baby girl," he said.

"Yes, my daughter, Kristy."

"I guess I wasn't expecting her to answer the phone. She sounds so grown up . . . not like a baby at all," he said.

"Nathan hasn't seen her for a long time," Danielle explained.

"Is she as beautiful as you are?" he asked.

Danielle looked at her daughter, who was already busy with her doll house again. "Much more so," she said.

"I find that impossible to believe."

"I have the figures on your addition," Danielle said, changing the subject. His voice and his words sounded so intimate, they were making her nervous. She quoted the price to him.

"Sounds reasonable. When will you start?" he asked.

"I'll have someone free in a couple of days."

"Will you be doing any of the work?" he asked hopefully.

"More than likely. We're several people short right now."

"That makes me very happy, Danielle. I'll have a part of you close to me all the time."

"Peter, I hardly think we know—"

"I intend to remedy that as soon as I get back," he interrupted.

"I've been thinking about our dinner date," Danielle began.

"And you've found out the evening you'll be free, right?" he interrupted again.

Danielle sighed. She'd intended to tell him that she'd decided against going. "You said you'd be back in ten days. I'll have an evening free that weekend," she said, then wondered why she'd agreed.

"I'll call you as soon as I get back."

"Good luck with your horse-buying," she said.

"Good luck with your bid on Valverde."

"Good night, Peter."

"Sweet dreams, Danielle Britton."

4

The sleek gray Cadillac Eldorado glided down the mountain road, its two occupants silent. For Danielle the past two weeks had flown by too quickly and the dreaded Saturday night had arrived too soon. It was almost like waiting for the other shoe to drop, just as it was with waiting for Beverly's next move, which apparently hadn't yet been made. Each event had its own portent of disaster.

The scene at the house, when Peter had come to pick her up, had been one of excitement and confusion. Penny had managed to get Kristy as enthusiastic about meeting the famed rodeo star as she was herself. To Danielle's credit, Kristy behaved like a lady, shaking hands and saying, "I'm very pleased to meet you, sir." Penny had simply gushed, the compliments flowing from her like water over a fall.

Peter deserved some credit too. He'd stayed calm in an obviously alien, child-inhabited home environment, and had graciously endured all the attention that was forced on him. He'd even sat down before the fire in the living room and held Kristy on his lap while she explained the intricacies of constructing handmade dolls such as Bizzy and rocking chairs such as the one she sat in.

Danielle had watched them from the kitchen doorway and realized that Kristy was immediately and completely taken with him. Peter told her about a Shetland pony who lived at his ranch and invited her to come out and ride him sometime. Kristy was delighted with the prospect and wasted no time in telling him that her mother could ride a horse.

For a moment while watching them Danielle felt sorry for her fatherless little girl. She tried to imagine what it would be like to have a man in the house, a man who'd sit by the fire and hold his daughter in his lap on cool October evenings like this one. The idea was preposterous, she decided, but it still hadn't left her mind.

"You look very beautiful tonight," Peter said as he turned south onto State Highway 14.

"Thank you," Danielle said. Her hair had turned out to be less of a problem than she thought it would. It was simply swept back on one side from an off-center part and fastened with a small gold clip. The rest hung loosely down her back with a soft curl at the ends. She'd had a hard time deciding what to wear. After searching her closet, she'd finally come up with something she thought she would be comfortable in.

The vicuña-colored suede skirt was full and flowing from the stitched-down pleats at the waist and tied with a belt of the same material. Her tucked-in sweater was of soft, cream wool with a wide side-split cowl collar. The simple, unadorned boots she wore exactly matched her skirt.

"You look like one of those models in the fashion magazines," he said. "I suppose you've thought about being a model, haven't you?"

"My mother thought about it for me. I never really had any interest in it."

"You seem happy with what you do," he said.

"Most of the time," she answered truthfully.

"What makes you unhappy about it?" he asked.

"Losing a bid is no fun," she answered.

"And have you? Lost a bid, I mean."

"Valverde," she said flatly.

Peter was silent for a moment. While he couldn't exactly relate to the distress she must be experiencing, he could sympathize with the feeling of loss. "It's tough when you don't get to do something you want to do very badly," he said. "There were a lot of other things for me to do with the ranch and the cattle and all, but when I took that last fall and found out I'd never ride again, I was pretty depressed."

"I imagine that must have been an awful time for you," Danielle said. "How did it happen?"

"They couldn't get the bull away from me fast enough. I think the old rogue had it in for me. He just kicked the hell out of my leg."

"Do you miss the rodeo very much?" she asked.

"I have a lot more to look forward to now than I ever did on the circuit. The ranch is a full-time job, now that I've got my kids."

"Your kids?" Danielle asked.

"We run a camp, full time in the summer, a few weekends during the rest of the year . . . if the weather's good." He glanced at her, smiling. "Wild Weston's Rancheros. We teach kids all about horses."

"That must be quite a handful, but it sounds like fun," Danielle said.

"It is. And the kids don't stay long enough to be any trouble. Six weeks is our longest camping term. They probably wait till they get home to raise a ruckus."

"So you really don't miss the rodeo?" Danielle asked thoughtfully.

"Not anymore. When I think back, it probably couldn't have happened at a better time. Six years ago I was thirty and already struggling to keep up with the younger fellows. It was just a matter of time before I lost it all one way or another."

Danielle was silent for a moment. It had been just about six years ago that she'd "lost it all" too. Had he been as devastated as she? she wondered. How much of a brave man's pride was attached to performing death-defying feats of masculine skill? She knew firsthand how much of a woman's pride was involved in being able to conceive and carry a child. Peter reached out and took her hand.

"Losing Valverde has you upset, doesn't it?" he asked.

"We've lost contracts before," she said.

"But nothing this big, am I right?"

"You're right," she conceded.

In silence they drove the rest of the way down and around the mountain to the Desert Gazer on the foothills of the other side. Peter held her hand all the way, and it somehow comforted her. She'd wrestled with her various problems alone for so long that it was rather pleasant to be in the company of someone who seemed to share her concern.

The Desert Gazer sat high enough on the southeastern outskirts of Albuquerque so that each room had a breathtaking view of the city and the beautiful desert that surrounded it on the other three sides. The long, C-shaped building was done in the southwestern style, made of adobe and white stucco with high, beamed ceilings and a fireplace in every cozy room.

As soon as they were seated the waiter brought champagne to the table and took their order.

"What's the occasion?" Danielle asked when the waiter had poured the wine and left them.

"Our first date," Peter said, and held his glass toward hers for a toast. "The first of many," he said.

Danielle hesitated, took a tiny sip, then looked out the window. She'd planned for this to be their last date as well. She couldn't ever remember being so uncomfortable in the presence of a man. It wasn't the annoyance of being teased or the malaise of loneliness. The disquietude seemed to stem from an uneasiness of her spirit and a discomposure of her thoughts. She felt totally out of touch with the dating scene and everything that she associated with it—the easy repartee, the provocative asides that made a person interesting.

Peter looked especially handsome tonight, she thought as she turned from the window, although he seemed a little uneasy also. He was facing the window, staring silently out at the city lights below them. He wore a jacket of fawn-colored suede cut in the western style and wool trousers of the same color. His white shirt looked strangely bright next to his deeply tanned skin. In profile the firm angles of his face were dramatically masculine and lovely to look at. She decided to make it as pleasant an evening as she possibly could.

"Did you enjoy your trip to San Antonio?" she asked.

"I made a good buy on a mare," he said, facing her again. "As for enjoying the trip, I would have enjoyed it a lot more if you'd been with me. San Antonio is nice this time of year."

"Nice and warm if I remember right," she said, ignoring his reference to wanting her with him.

Peter nodded. "Do you remember the river walk downtown?" he asked.

"It's lovely," she said.

"Not if you're alone."

Danielle looked at him for a moment and sipped at her wine. His expression was serious, his implication disconcerting. "So, what else did you find to do while you were there?" she asked.

"I bought some fixtures for the store and visited an aunt and uncle of mine. That's about all . . . except for this." He reached into a pocket of his jacket and brought out a piece of leather. "I worked on this at night," he said and handed it to her.

"Peter, this is lovely," she said. The fine leather oval had been carefully cut and hand-tooled to form an ornament for the hair. The piece was pierced through either end with one carved pin of cherry wood.

"It's something you can use," he said modestly. "It doesn't seem like much of a gift . . . after seeing what you've done to my bedroom." He shook his head. "Remarkable." The word was almost whispered.

"You're pleased, then?" she asked.

"More than that: I can't imagine how I stood the room any other way." The waiter served their salads, then poured more wine. When he left, Peter continued. "Tell me what work you personally did on it, will you?"

"It started out with drawings," she said.

"Drawings that you did?" he asked.

Danielle nodded. "Sally did the estimate, the wrecking crew tore out the wall—"

"The wrecking crew?" he asked.

"We have two young men who especially like to do that sort of thing and are really good at it. We call them the wrecking crew," she explained. "I bought all the materials, then another mason and I did the concrete and adobe work after the forms and supports were built."

"I expected the whole thing to be a real mess, but it wasn't," he said.

"We're proud of that. It's one of the things that sets us apart from the rest," she said.

"The woman's touch," he said softly.

Danielle had never examined her motives for insisting that a work site be kept clean, even if people had to work overtime to do it. She knew it was good business—but the "woman's touch"? Was that really what it was? she wondered.

"I imagine you can take the credit for all that," Peter

said. When Danielle nodded, he went on: "I want you to tell me how you came to be a general contractor."

She told Peter that at the age of eleven she'd begun working beside her father in one capacity or another. A "go-fer" at first, she'd soon learned the rudiments of wiring and carpentry mostly by observation. In spite of some resistance and objection from a few of his tradesmen, Danielle had been allowed to work alongside the male crew. Boyd Britton let it be known that he'd fire anyone who wouldn't cooperate with his daughter's apprenticeship.

It was soon obvious to all that Danni was willing to work as hard as they, and a comfortable rapport was finally enjoyed among all of them. In the next seven years before she left for college, she was very close to becoming a journeyman carpenter, plumber, electrician and mason.

In college Danielle had majored in architecture and minored in business with the idea that she would work with a local architectural firm after graduation and help her father with his books when he needed her. It didn't happen that way, however. Boyd needed her skills as a tradesman when she returned, and within the next year she took her tests in Santa Fe and became fully licensed in several areas of construction.

Danielle mentioned her marriage but didn't go into any details. She said nothing about her unsuccessful pregnancy, the disastrous nature of her divorce or the circumstances surrounding Kristy's adoption.

"Sounds like my background," Peter said, and leaned back so that the waiter could serve them. "Learning by doing. It's a hard road, isn't it?"

"There can be some pretty rough patches," Danielle said.

"Speaking of a rough patch," Peter whispered, "here comes a friend of mine."

"Peter Weston, you old cowpuncher. How in hell have

you been?" In one fluid motion a wiry young man slapped Peter on the back, pulled out a chair and sat down while the waiter serving their meal worked around him as best he could. The man glanced at Danielle, seeing her for the first time, and immediately stood up again, almost tipping his chair. "Pardon me, ma'am." He swept his cowboy hat off his head and held it to his thin chest.

Peter's smile was wide. "This is Danielle Britton . . . Hubert Netter."

Danielle started to reach for his hand, then thought better of it. The man was making a slight bow in her direction and obviously didn't expect a woman to shake hands.

"I'm honored, ma'am," he said. "Pleased to make your acquaintance."

"Thank you," she said as he sat down again.

Hubert turned to Peter again. "I tried to call you last week, but Art said you were down in Texas. I had to tell you the good news. Jenny and I are gettin' married," he said excitedly, sitting on the edge of the chair.

"She finally said yes. Well, congratulations, Hubie." Peter shook Hubert's hand and Hubert beamed.

"Three years I been courtin' that woman," Hubie said. "Finally figured out what she wanted."

"What was that?" Peter asked as he started to cut into his steak.

"Romance," he said. "You know me, an explosion lookin' for a place to happen. I just had to slow down a bit—you know, take my time with things."

"I'm happy for you, Hubie," Peter said.

"Yes, congratulations . . . and good luck," Danielle said.

Hubert Netter stood up abruptly. "Gotta go. Got a meeting."

"He really is an explosion, isn't he?" Danielle said when Hubie had left.

"Bronco rider. Guess some of the horse rubs off," Peter said with a smile.

They decided that their steaks were perfect, and the champagne had relaxed Danielle to the point where she could enjoy her meal. When they'd walked in, she was sure she wouldn't be able to eat a bite of anything. But the previous nervousness seemed to have vanished, just as Hubie Netter had.

"Hubie reminds me of my father," Danielle said. "Always busy. It makes a marriage difficult."

"They'll need some luck all right. Hubie's place is smaller than mine, but he's just as busy. I can't imagine how he's going to do it, especially if they have children."

"Children do take a lot of time," Danielle agreed.

"Lots of responsibility."

"Yes," she agreed again, then remembered his earlier comment about children raising a ruckus at home. "But they're worth it," she added.

"I wouldn't know about that," he said, sounding skeptical. "I enjoy having them around during camp."

"Then you can ship them home before they make any trouble for you," Danielle said softly.

Peter immediately sensed her negative reaction to the implications he'd said. "I guess I'm a little bit cynical about marriage and children." He put down his fork and leaned forward. "I still think my parents split up because of me. There just doesn't seem to be enough romance in the world, and marriage seems to destroy what little there is."

Danielle couldn't dispute what he was saying. Romance seemed like a delicate flower: Once cut off from its source of nourishment it died. There were two things that could happen, she thought. The flower could be discarded and the plant tended with the hope that it would produce another bloom. In the case of her parents and many of her acquaintances, the plant was not tended well enough. The more desirable alternative would be to tend the plant and save the flower. Even crispy-dry, its petals would offer up their lovely fragrance to be enjoyed by those who wished to keep the essence alive in their hearts.

"Tell me what you're thinking about," Peter said.

She waited until their dishes had been cleared away and their coffee poured, then hesitantly told him what she'd just been musing over.

"That's a beautiful way to look at it," he said. "Maybe the real problem is that nobody knows exactly what nourishes the flower."

"I've never figured it out," she said.

"I'm not sure anyone can," he said.

She didn't want to argue, and her parents were truly a case in point. "Maybe you're right," Danielle said. "My parents have problems because my father's too busy to think about romance. I wish I could help, but . . ."

"How would you help?" Peter asked curiously when she trailed off.

Danielle told him about how she'd planned to send them on a cruise if she'd won the Valverde contract. "I wanted to get them away from here long enough to get my father's mind off work, but I guess I'll just have to come up with something else."

Peter reached for her hand. "It sounds like you're the romantic one in the family, Danielle," he said.

The lovely oval of leather lay to her right, and she picked it up. "I think you may have a romantic streak, too, Peter Weston." The wine was making her unusually brave.

His eyes caught hers. "You're the only person who's ever said that to me, Danni. It's been an easy secret to keep—until now." He gave her hand a gentle squeeze.

"Why would you want to keep it a secret?" she asked.

"The more someone knows about you, the more vulnerable you are. It has a lot to do with trusting the other person . . . feeling comfortable with them."

Danielle couldn't respond to the compliment he'd just given her. When she'd thought about him over the past two weeks, it had been with mistrust in her heart. She'd pondered again and again the unusual circumstances of their various meetings, then decided to find out for certain.

In a casual conversation Nathan had told her that their introduction had been an innocent plan of his own to bring two seemingly compatible friends together. Peter's visit to the mortgage company Boyd Britton worked for was completely logical: They'd held the first mortgage on his ranch and therefore would be the best place to get a second. Danielle's father had assured her that he'd not mentioned that she would be at Valverde on the day Peter arrived there. Still, she couldn't quite trust his interest in her.

The waiter arrived with the check and Danielle excused herself. Alone in the ladies' room, she stared at her reflection in the mirror. Her life was busy and full; most of the time it was a happy existence, but it was lacking in one area. She'd enjoyed herself tonight, she decided as she combed her hair unnecessarily. Perhaps having a man for a friend wouldn't be so bad.

Just because one disastrous marriage had threatened to ruin her life didn't mean she'd have to plunge into another. Peter had all but said that he wasn't the marrying kind, never had been. It was unlikely that he ever would be. Was it safe to hope that they could be friends, even lovers, and avoid the romantic trap and its eventual painful demise? she wondered. Was a casual relationship possible? It probably wasn't, she decided as she returned to the table.

"More coffee?" he asked as she sat down.

"Not another thing," she said, sighing with satisfaction. "Everything was wonderful. Thank you."

"Do you have to go right home?" he asked.

"Well . . ."

"Tomorrow's Sunday. You're off aren't you?"

"Yes . . . but . . ."

"I'd like to show you something," he said.

"What is it?" she asked.

"I'd like to keep it a surprise. Do you mind?"

Danielle shrugged, then smiled. "I like surprises."

"That settles it, then."

Danielle thought he might have been thinking of taking her dancing, but they returned to the state highway and were soon traveling north on the road to his ranch. The wine was dictating her composure at the moment, but there was an undercurrent of apprehension lurking in the back of her mind. She was surprised when they passed by the main house, then turned east again.

Around a curve and behind a small knoll, they came upon a series of rustic-looking wooden buildings and split-rail fences that looked more like Danielle's idea of a ranch than the main house. Peter pointed out two bunk houses, one for the hands and one for the young campers. In addition to the large barn there were also two long, low stables and a few other outbuildings.

Peter pulled the Cadillac up to one end of the nearest stable and stopped. In the next moment he was out of the car and opening her door for her. "Right this way, ma'am," he said, bowing low.

Danielle accompanied him through a gate, then toward the end stall. The light was on, showing brightly through the open upper half of the door. A soft whickering sound could be heard as they approached.

"How's she doing, Katz?" Peter asked, looking inside.

A girl of about fourteen, standing on the opposite side of the horse, peered beneath the animal's neck, then stepped under it. "Hi, Pete. She's still a little nervous, but I've been talking to her for the last half hour."

"Is it helping?" Peter asked.

76

"I think so," Katz said. "But I'm gonna sleep out here just in case."

"Your dad said it was okay?" Peter asked.

"Oh, sure. No problem."

"Danni Britton, meet Katherine Dobbs. Best hand on the place . . . except maybe for her father."

"You have a beautiful horse, Katherine," Danielle said.

"Call me, Katz," she said. "This is Pete's new horse, Calamity Queen. Mine's not nearly so skittish. Hey! Look at that!"

Calamity Queen had turned and was cautiously edging up to the doorway. She gave Danielle a thorough looking-over, flared her nostrils and sniffed the air, then gently nuzzled Danielle's shoulder with her soft lips.

"Well, I'll be," Katz said incredulously. "She's backed up from everybody 'cept you and me today, Pete."

Danielle looked at Peter. "This is a very nice surprise," she said. "Thank you."

"I thought you'd like her. Especially after what I heard from Kristy tonight. Sounded like you're just about the best rider in the world."

"Kristy exaggerates quite a bit," Danielle said as she brought her hand up slowly to touch Calamity's neck.

"Now that you've seen her, do you think you'd like to ride her sometime?" Peter asked.

"Yes, I think I would," she said happily.

"Then it's settled. We have a date." Peter gave Katz a pat on the shoulder. "You're a swell kid, Katz. You have a good night."

"Calamity's fine company, Pete. Don't worry about me."

"This was very nice of you, Peter," Danielle said when they were back in the car. "A very thoughtful thing to do."

"You mean it's showing again?" he asked.

"What?"

"My romantic nature?"

Danielle smiled. "I guess your secret's out for sure. You'd better be careful—someone will take advantage of you."

"I hope so . . . as long as it's you."

Danielle was afraid to respond. She glanced out the windshield and to her left. "Oh . . . that does look nice," she said. Coming from the opposite direction, she hadn't noticed the new addition to Peter's bedroom. Now she could see it clearly.

A light was on inside, and where there'd been blank wall before, there was now a wide archway opening onto a glassed-in porch that ran the full length of the room. Three matching arches made up the outer wall of the porch, the center arch wider than the two on either side. The view from inside, she knew, was lovely.

"It's perfect," he said. "What say we celebrate? A glass of brandy before I take you home."

"It's getting kind of late," she said.

"Tomorrow's Sunday, remember?"

She took another look at her work as they turned back south. "That's right, it is," she said, and wasn't sure whether Danielle or the wine was talking.

Wood for a fire had already been laid in the living-room fireplace, and it took only a short time to get a blaze started. On her first visit Danielle had been so uncomfortable, she hadn't noticed the beauty of the room and its furnishings. She did so now while Peter finished with the fire, then poured their snifters of brandy at a bar in the far corner of the room.

The fireplace was of natural stone, probably taken right from the property itself. The floor was the same parquet as the bedroom; the walls were rough white stucco, and the high beams of the ceiling were dark and rich. Including those in his bedroom, Peter had an exceptional collection of American Indian rugs. Even in so vast a room they created a cozy feeling of intimate spaces and luxurious variety.

Danielle was feeling a bit awkward. The fire was beginning to crackle and blaze. From somewhere near the bar Peter had dimmed the lights and was returning to the couch in front of the fireplace. The setting was dark, warm and romantic, and Danielle realized she had no idea what to do next. She put her hands into the side pockets of her skirt for lack of a better thing to do with them, and found the gift Peter had given her.

"Thank you again for this," she said, taking it from her pocket. "You do beautiful work."

Peter put the brandy on the coffee table, then came forward. "I'm glad you like it," he said, putting his hands on her waist. He gazed at her intently for a moment; then he asked suddenly: "Have you ever been in love?"

"Yes," she said softly. "I was once."

"What went wrong?"

"Many things," she answered.

"I'm frightened of love, aren't you?" Peter asked quietly.

For some unknown reason Danielle felt a tightening in her throat and the sting of approaching tears. All she could do was nod her agreement.

Peter pulled her close to him. In his arms he held a talented, highly skilled and successful woman who appeared to need no one. But somewhere in his heart he knew she could be just as fragile as anyone. The desire to protect her was overwhelming—but what would he be protecting her from? he wondered. She shielded herself very well from the world outside her work.

"You're a very special woman, Danni," he said. "And you're so special to me."

"Peter . . ." she started to protest. Then his lips were melting on hers, his hands holding her fast against his firm body. The heat of the summer desert seemed to fill the room: She could feel it from the top of her head to the tip of her toes.

That first kiss, two weeks before, had only hinted at what was to come. The gentleness that had made her light-headed then was now a hunger that made her weak with desire. Her lips gladly opened to the provocative invitation of his tongue. His tentative explorations were tender, but his arms held her fiercely, her body crushed against him as if she might fall if he let her go.

Danielle lifted her hands to his shoulders, her left still clutching the beautiful ornament he'd made for her hair. The tooled leather felt rough under her thumb, and she rubbed at it, as if concentrating on it could take her mind off what was happening to her body. It could not.

Her long-denied passions were becoming ungovernable, her mind embarking on flights of fantasy in the arms of a man who could love her. Peter Weston, the man with the romantic streak, the man who was frightened of love, was stealing her heart. She felt utterly possessed.

5

His lips began to tease her, nibbling, taunting, moving from chin to cheek to ear. A gentle biting at her earlobe sent shivers of pleasure through her body. Strong fingers were rubbing up her spine, causing her to arch toward him, and she offered no resistance.

"So special," he murmured, his hand brushing at her hair, his desire-darkened eyes on hers. "I'm glad Nathan brought us together, Danni. I can't imagine my life without knowing you."

Danielle leaned slightly away. "Do you really think you know me that well, Peter?"

"I know you're the most exciting woman I've ever met. I know that you're beautiful, and talented, and . . ."

A finger silenced him.

"Why do my compliments bother you, Danni?" he asked. "I sensed it even on the night we met."

As surely as she knew her name, Danielle knew that her own image of herself made her uncomfortable with praise, except where her work or her daughter was concerned. "I thought you were trying to make up for your mistake," she said. "I didn't think you meant any of it."

"I've never been a hypocrite, Danni. I'd never deceive you." Then he smiled, took her hand and led her to the couch. "I think I've been rushing things too much," he said as they sat down.

A smile crossed Danielle's face as he handed her a brandy snifter. "Maybe you should consider slowing down—like Hubert did," she teased him, then took a sip of the strong wine.

"I will . . . if you'll promise to marry me," he said.

Danielle barely kept from choking as she swallowed the fiery liquid. A frown crossed her face as she looked at him. She couldn't believe what he'd said, nor could she believe that he'd meant it. "I was right," she said. "You're doing it again."

"Doing what?" he asked.

"Saying things you don't mean, just like you did the night we met."

"I've meant every word I've ever said to you, Danni," he said seriously.

"Peter, please . . ." She was almost to the point of anger. "It's hard enough to believe that I'm here," she blurted out.

Peter turned toward her with an undefinable look on his face. "You mean I'm not your type," he said flatly.

"No! That's not it at all."

"Then what do you mean?" he asked, his hand sliding behind her on the couch.

"It's just that . . ." The glass she held was twisting around in her nervous hands as she stared down at it. "It just seems that . . . I'm not anybody's type." Had she really said it? she wondered. She'd never felt more vulnerable in all her life.

His eyes were on her—she could feel them—but he

didn't say anything right away. To keep from crushing the glass in her hand, she lifted it to her lips and took a long draft. The amber liquid burned her tongue and her throat, then filled her body with a rush of unaccustomed warmth.

Peter took the glass from her hand and put it on the coffee table alongside his. One hand came back to rest on her waist, the other across her shoulders, and he kissed her cheek. "Thank heaven I met you when I did," he said softly into her ear. "I'm a lucky man."

"Peter . . ." She could feel him removing the gold clip from her hair.

"Don't say any more," he commanded as he took possession of her lips again.

Danielle felt her body weaken and she relaxed back against the cushion. She heard the gold hair clip drop against the wood of the table behind the couch, then his hand was behind her head, his fingers sinking into her thick hair.

The romantic setting, the wine, the warmth of the fire, seemed to combine in a conspiracy against her will to resist the temptation of Peter Weston. *Caution* was a word that flitted through her mind, and left as quickly as it had come. She welcomed every touch of his lips, every caress of his hands, as evidence of her desirability. It didn't even matter that he was undoing the buttons along one shoulder of her sweater.

He touched her almost reverently but without hesitation, one hand moving over the soft angora of her sweater, the other slipping inside the opening at the unbuttoned shoulder. Her own fingers crept around his waist and pressed into the firm flesh. She could feel him trembling as he outlined the high, round shape of her upturned breasts through the fine wool. No bra restrained them, and Peter sighed with pleasure at their response.

Strong fingers tugged at the soft material and soon

found their way beneath it at her waist. The heat of his touch against her slender midriff seared through her as no wine could. The hand over her shoulder moved back and forth across her collarbone, then stopped and began a slow descent on its way to meet the other. She gasped and dug her fingers into the muscles of his back as he found a peak of fire awaiting his touch.

"That's it," he whispered against her cheek. "Hold on to me. Don't ever stop holding on, Danni. I'm right here for you."

She sought his lips, the wine-sweet taste urging her on to daring ventures. Her hunger for him was mounting with every breath she took, his lush, male fragrance filling her lungs with the energy of long-forgotten passion. His words became a song of invitation as inquiring fingers spread across his chest, the pearl snaps of his shirt opening with little persuasion.

Still his hands caressed her, his hard fingers exploring soft, forbidden contours, then gently brushing, pinching. Her mouth opened beneath his, a low moan escaping her trembling lips.

With a single smooth motion Peter slipped both hands beneath her sweater at the waist and raised it over her head. He held her face in his hands then, smoothing her heavy hair, kissing her cheeks. She could feel his hands move to her bare back as his tongue began its probing search for sweet tastes and hidden fires. Without surrendering her lips, he urged her onto his lap, then nestled her back against a corner full of soft pillows.

It felt so good to be held by strong arms, to be caressed by sensitive hands, to be explored with kisses. His tongue moved mysteriously over her heated flesh, as if searching for a treasure—until he found it. One tingling nipple surged with vibrant life as he tugged it into his mouth. A cry of exquisite pleasure escaped her as he found the other and drew sparks of lightning through her awakened body. Her fingers dug into the muscles of his arms, the pulses of pleasure so intense that she could barely control her clutching hands or gasping breath.

Soft kisses trailed between her breasts, then the touch of his lips was gone. For a moment she lay with her eyes closed, trying to regain some of her composure, until she realized he was looking at her. She tried to rise, but strong hands on her shoulders held her against the cushions.

"You look like a beautiful goddess," he said, then let one finger follow a long tendril of her hair as it lay across her shoulder, the curling end just touching the swelling peak of her breast. "So beautiful," he whispered, his finger now at the end of its journey, pushing the heavy curl aside, focusing his attention on the jutting point.

"No . . ."

"Yes. I want you to listen to me. I want you to hear how I feel." His hand left her breast and moved to the belt of her skirt. "Maybe you don't believe me now, but you will—because I'm not going to stop telling you how beautiful you are to me."

In a moment, under his gentle ministrations, she wore nothing at all except the flickering light of the fire. He cradled her close to him. "I have the world in my arms," he murmured. "Don't be afraid, Danni."

Her hand, pressing against the soft curling hair on his chest, pulsed with his heartbeat. She leaned forward, her long hair falling like a satin curtain across her shoulders and breasts as she focused on her task. His shirt soon lay on the floor beside her skirt, but she could go no further. Once again she was shy and afraid.

She drew her knees up slightly and sat staring straight ahead, her hair hiding her expression of bewilderment and indecision. There were so many things she wanted to say to him. How else could he know that he, too, was beautiful to her? How else could he know that she wanted him to make love to her?

Before she could comprehend what was happening,

she was in his arms, he was standing, turning, then she was being lowered to the soft pillows of the couch. In the next moment he was easing his tall frame down beside her, his hard, unclothed body pressing against her.

She hadn't been able to watch him finish undressing, but now she looked at him. The splendor of his male body was bathed in firelight, his need for her unquestionable.

"Say you believe me now," he whispered, and waited for her to answer. His hand brushed lightly over her stomach, then down the top of her thigh.

Too many days of loneliness kept her silent. She turned into his arms and kissed him. Even in the darkened room she felt shy and awkward.

Peter sensed her unease and simply held her for a time, his hands gently caressing her, marveling at her slender beauty, her silent strength. His efforts were not in vain. She relaxed in his arms; her hands began to touch him again, their movement across his skin bringing him closer and closer to the ultimate question. He wanted her to be as hungry for him as he was for her.

"I wanted this to happen the night I met you," he said candidly.

Danielle frowned.

"Remember when you said that the bed seemed to be in the perfect place?"

She nodded.

"I almost said, 'It's the perfect place for you.'"

Danielle remembered the incident; she'd glanced at the bed. "You had a funny look on your face when I turned back to you," she said.

"Do you wonder why? You were in my bedroom, talking business, and business was the farthest thing from my mind. I wanted to lock the door and make love to you."

"Now I know you're teasing me," she said.

"Your naiveté is lovely, Danni. You really don't realize

your effect on men, do you? There wasn't a man here that night who didn't try to bribe me out of your phone number."

"Why would they do that?" she asked.

"Maybe they were thinking the same thing I was," he said with a smile.

"And what was that?" she asked.

"Maybe they were thinking how beautiful you'd look in the firelight," he said, his hand moving over her breasts, then down her side. "Maybe they wanted to taste you." His tongue slowly circled one rosy nipple, then the other. "Maybe they wanted to feel your warm skin beneath their hands." A feathery touch glided over the curve of her hip, down the outside of her leg, then rose along her inner thigh.

"Peter . . ." Her body was throbbing with need, her erratic breathing almost uncontrollable.

"You asked me a question, Danni. Don't you want to hear the answer?"

All she could do was shake her head no.

"Ah, but I think you should hear it, Danni. You should know what men are thinking about when they look at you." As he spoke his fingers made lazy little circles on her inner thigh. "It's the same thing I was thinking the night I met you. I wanted to feel your body come alive when I touched you."

Danielle gripped his shoulders and gasped with surprise and pleasure when his hand moved higher. She arched toward him, her arms helplessly tightening around him, pulling him closer. An intense heat flared within her. "Peter, please!" she cried out.

"Come to me, Danni," he breathed as he lifted his body over hers.

Her legs were being pressed apart by his, opening the way to her secret life, her simmering hunger. She felt the touch of him, the mighty passion flaming at the gate of her emptiness. Her appetite for the intoxication of fulfill-

ment seemed a restless predator that demanded sustenance, and she arched against him.

Unbidden, a loud cry of joy issued from his lips. Peter
was lost within the persistent dream that had tormented
him since the day they'd met. He wanted to have control
over the frenzied storm that raged through his being,
but he didn't. Nor could he stay his continuous moans of
ecstasy as they moved together.

A moment before, she'd felt as empty and incomplete
as the vast cavern of Valverde, as truly naive as her
daughter, Kristy. Now she was beyond satiety, filled with
the extravagance of masculine passion, his lavish gift an
inordinate bounty that overwhelmed her and sent her
doubts flying.

She reveled in the luxury of his weight upon her, the
plunging need that met her urgent demands again and
again until she felt she would burst. The pleasure was
outrageous, flaming through her as she felt his arms
crushing her to him, her body now overflowing as the
sounds of their joyful release spiraled through the room.

He held her tightly, not moving from her, straining to
compose his thoughts while he kissed her tenderly.
Because of her illusive coolness, he hadn't suspected her
capacity for passion. For the first time in his life he knew
he'd found a woman who could make him fall in love and
be happy in doing so. Her power both intrigued and
frightened him. She'd seduced him without even trying;
he'd asked her to marry him before he'd realized the
words had formed in his mind. He was mystified, both by
her and his own reaction to her.

"Now you know what I was thinking," he murmured,
looking down into brightened eyes.

She smiled. "We were talking business," she teased
him.

"*You* were," he corrected. "I was imagining that I was
making love to you."

"And all the time I thought you were listening politely," she said.

"How could I?"

"I didn't tempt you," she said.

"That's easy for you to say." He smiled. "Have you ever watched yourself move? Have you ever looked into a mirror and seen how seductive those big blue eyes can be? You bewitched me. It's as simple . . . and as complicated as that."

Danielle's hands played lightly down his sides. "No one has ever said such outlandish things to me, Peter Weston. Are you sure you're in possession of all your senses?"

Peter eased himself onto his side and faced her. "Shall we test them?"

"If you're not afraid to find something missing," she said teasingly.

"I can see that you're a beautiful woman," he began, a finger brushing over her cheek, then descending her throat and coming to rest on her breast. "I heard you call my name." He kissed her lips, then nuzzled her ear. "Your fragrance delights me," he said, nipping softly at her earlobe.

The fondling of her breast as he talked was making her shiver with delight all over again. "Peter, maybe you'd better do this some other time," she said with quavering breath.

"What makes you so impatient with me?" he asked, smiling mischievously. "You're always wanting to go on to the next question before I've answered the first."

His tugging at the sensitive peak of her breast seemed to be an absently indulged pastime. He was speaking so casually, he might have been out for a Sunday stroll. "You've answered enough," she said. "I'll concede the point."

"But the test isn't complete. . . . There's taste . . ." he

went on, his hand slipping behind her back to lift her. His mouth closed over the tip of her breast, his teeth teasing with gentle pressure, his lips pulling at the tingling skin.

Danielle writhed in his arms, but he refused to relinquish his hold. Her words of argument were choked off in her throat as he drew a new fire through her veins. Each breath she took in left her in shuddering gasps of vibrant sound.

Again her wild response filled him with tremors of desire. He fought for control as he lifted his lips from her throbbing breast. His breathing began to slow, and hers did also as she lay back on the pillows. He thought he could go on with his exploring. His hand moved to her abdomen and smoothed the silken skin, then caught her wrist.

Danielle watched in amazement as he guided her hand. She heard the swift intake of his breath when she touched him and the harsh sigh of pleasure as he closed his hand over hers. She lay rigid with anticipation, her heart rapping ever faster against her chest. His lips hovered over hers, nibbling, caressing, as his hand moved back across her stomach, then lower.

The thrumming sound that assaulted her ears was her own voice as he found the path to her burning center. Unknowingly she grasped him, urging him on. Daggers of fire surged through her as he brought her forth again and she arched against him.

He thought to let her quiet for a moment, but she urged him over her again, breathing his name with a pleading sound. No longer the shy woman he'd brought there that night, Danielle moved to complete the union with the abandon of a nymph.

Peter felt his heart racing as if it would leave his chest. This woman was indeed the most exciting creature he'd ever known. His body was ablaze, throbbing mightily with every stroke, her cries the rhythm of their final freedom.

Exhausted, they clung to each other, their kisses of passion dissolving into kisses of tender care, then playfulness. Harmony had at last replaced the dissonance of that first meeting.

"Is there anything else you'd like to have me explain to you?" he asked, his tone languorous, his finger tracing lazily down her nose.

Danielle's expression was mischievous. "Have you been explaining something to me?" she asked.

"Danielle Britton," he warned menacingly.

"Well . . ." She propped herself up on her elbows. "If school's out, I guess I'd better be—"

"You'd better be nice to the teacher, that's what you'd better be."

"Or what? You'll stand me in the corner?"

"Oh, nothing like that," he said teasingly.

"What, then?"

He rolled onto his side and propped himself up on one elbow, his cheek against his open palm. "Since you haven't seen fit to listen while I was very patiently trying to answer your questions, I can always try what I had in mind the night we met."

"And that was . . . ?"

"I wanted to lock the door and keep you in my bed all night, remember?"

She spoke and gave a push at the same time. "You're impossible."

Peter's tall frame went rolling off the couch. "Hey! Is that any way to treat such a patient guy?" he said, looking back at her.

Danielle reached down from the couch and trailed a hand down his side. She peered over the edge as her fingers traced his hip, then her hand stopped abruptly. Beginning at the top of his thigh was an angry-looking red scar that ran almost to his knee.

"*Peter,*" her voice was soft with caring. "How did this happen?"

He pulled her on top of him. A light kiss stopped her heartfelt query.

"Are you all right now?" she asked softly.

"I've never been better." He smiled. "It's just a scar, Danielle."

"The bull?" she asked.

He nodded. "The last one." He held her face in his big hands. "Hey, don't look so worried. A few screws, a little hardware, Peter Weston's good as new."

Danielle kissed his palm. "Better than new, Mr. Weston." She kissed his lips. "Now, if I really haven't broken you in half, you'd better drive me home." She tried to get up, but he wouldn't let her.

"Only if you'll promise me one thing."

"What's that?"

"That you'll come back tomorrow and bring Kristy. I promised to introduce her to a pony of mine."

"Tomorrow is Sunday. . . ."

"Today is Sunday," he corrected, looking at his watch.

"Peter! I really do have to go."

He held her fast. "Then say you'll come back."

"For a little while," she said finally. "In the afternoon." She'd never felt so wonderfully tired in her life.

Kristy's meeting with the Shetland, Gimlet, was a complete success. Peter's patient way with children put the little girl right at ease. He let her help with everything from putting on the tiny saddle to currying the brown and white pony when they were through with riding.

For days after their meeting, Gimlet and Peter were all Kristy could talk about. She'd tell anyone who'd listen to her, even strangers on the phone, and Bizzy was told everything in great detail, over and over again.

The work on the Belmonde tract of small houses proceeded on schedule, even though Danielle was often short handed and had to leave the office frequently and pitch in. In the evening she'd come home exhausted and fall into bed at the same time Kristy did. She and Peter spoke every day on the phone, but with their conflicting schedules they couldn't seem to find the time to get together.

By the Saturday after their dinner date, Calamity Queen had taken ill. Peter or Katz stayed with her around the clock most days, and when Peter called Danielle at night, he'd sound exhausted too.

For three more weeks their schedules collided, their phone calls the only solace in a never-ending round of commitments. Just when Danielle thought she was going to get a Sunday off, Jay Humphry's workers walked off the job at Valverde.

"It's wonderful and it's terrible," she told Peter. "I'm going to put another bid together, just in case."

"On Sunday, right?" he asked.

"Uh-huh," she said.

"Need some help?" he asked.

"Roberta and Sally said they'd come in," she said before she realized what he was suggesting.

"Will they mind if we lock them out of the office for a while?"

By the sound of his voice she could tell he was smiling. "They wouldn't mind a bit, cowboy."

"Are you in bed?" he asked.

"Yes."

"Alone?"

"Peter!"

"This is driving me crazy, Danni. I'm spending another night in a stable and I don't know how much longer I can stand not seeing you."

"Shall I come out to the stable, Peter?" she teased.

"Would you? Would you really do that?"

Although she'd been teasing a moment before, Danielle made an instant decision. "Does a horse have ears?"

"How soon can you be here?" he asked excitedly.

"I'll have to call Penny and see if she's free."

"Call me right back and tell me," he said.

But it wasn't to be: Penny was busy. Peter was good-natured about it and asked Danielle to send him a picture of herself so he could remember what she looked like. On Monday morning she put one in the mail, but he didn't receive it for two weeks. The uncle he'd visited in San Antonio died on Sunday night, and Peter left for Texas the next morning.

Danielle felt lonely despite the fact that she was busier than ever. To win the Valverde contract, which was open again because of Humphry's walkout, she was forced to include a close-to-impossible completion date in her bid.

On the day she received notice that Britton had won the contract, Danielle heard from Beverly through her lawyer. She'd filed suit for custody of Kristy. Danielle successfully kept her worry from her daughter, but even getting the Valverde contract couldn't lift her spirits. Peter still called her every night from San Antonio, but she couldn't bring herself to share her anxiety with him. For some reason she wasn't ready for him to know Kristy's story.

On the day Peter was to return from Texas, Danielle made an astounding discovery: Humphry's electrical wiring at Valverde had not been done in compliance with the municipal code. As it stood, it was not only illegal, it was also a safety hazard.

"What did you do?" Peter asked when he called late that evening.

"Sally and I inspected the whole job. The problem's consistent throughout Humphry's work."

"Does Emmitt French know?" Peter asked.

"Emmitt's the second one I called. Park Menendez was first."

"Is Park in any kind of trouble?"

"That remains to be seen. I hope not. He's one of the nicest people on earth."

"What's French going to do about it?"

"Emmitt thinks Park can force Humphry to fix it."

"Do you think he can?" he asked.

"No. Humphry hasn't got anyone left to do the work."

"I guess Boyd was right about Humphry's bid. There really was something fishy about it."

"Dad usually is right about anything to do with general contracting," she said.

Peter paused for a moment, then said, "Tomorrow's Sunday."

"Is it?" she asked. She truly didn't know. A letter from Beverly lay beside her on the bed.

"I'm coming in to see Nathan in the morning. What will you be doing in the afternoon?"

"Waiting to see you," she said.

"So Valverde's had another setback, has it?" Nathan chuckled as he carried the coffee pot to the kitchen table. "Couldn't happen to a nicer fellow," Nathan said sarcastically.

"I take it you don't like Emmitt French," Peter said.

"Shall we say he's just a wee bit off the straight and narrow. He deserved Humphry and the trouble."

"I'm just hoping this doesn't cause too much trouble for Danni," Peter said.

"I think you should worry a little about yourself, too, Peter," Nathan said as he poured coffee for both of them.

"Why's that, Nathan?"

"Have you signed anything locking in your interest rate on that loan you want to get?"

"It's kind of early for that, don't you think?" Peter asked. "Besides, no loan company in their right mind would guarantee a rate right now unless they had some pretty good evidence that Valverde would be completed on schedule." Peter drummed his fingers on the table.

"Danni refuses to go on with the work until Humphry's problem is fixed . . . and she doesn't see how he can possibly redo the job. He doesn't have the people."

"If Humphry's men had gone on strike, French would be stuck with it. But since the people are unorganized and simply walking off the job, for whatever reasons, Menendez can hire somebody else to do the work over again," Nathan said.

"But that'll cost him, Nathan. That's probably why he's insisting he can force Humphry to get back in there."

"What's Danni going to do in the meantime?" Nathan asked.

"She's already revised her original contract and is ready to do the work as soon as Park Menendez says go. But who knows when that'll be."

"Exactly my point. All Boyd Britton can do is wait and see."

Peter shook his head. "And interest rates aren't going to stay down in the basement like they are right now." He was silent for a moment and sipped at his coffee. "You know what, Nathan? I could be in a lot of trouble here."

"How's that, Peter?"

"I've sunk every bit of my profit back into the ranch and the Rancheros. I look great on paper, but . . ." He grinned. "You want to talk cash-flow problems, Nathan? If I figure on the worst interest rate and no profit from the store for four months, we're talking cash-flow disaster, good buddy."

"I suppose you could try playing your trump card," Nathan said.

"What are you talking about, Nathan?"

"Boyd Britton *is* Danni's father . . ." Nathan said suggestively, a wide grin on his face. "I'm sure he thinks that Danni and Kristy both need a man around the house."

Peter picked up the coffee pot and poured. He was

almost sure that Nathan was kidding. They both cared for Danielle Britton, and his suggestion had to be a joke. Still, Peter felt angry that Nathan had even thought of such a thing.

"What makes Boyd think those two need a man around?" he asked. "They seem perfectly happy the way things are. You know that as well as anybody."

"Maybe I do . . . and maybe they are," Nathan said skeptically.

"There's nothing a man can do that Danni can't," Peter said.

"Isn't there?"

Nathan's allusive tone immediately brought back the memory of their night together. Peter put on a weak smile. "I know you're joshing, Nat, but seriously . . . I don't think Danni has marriage in mind, not now, maybe not ever."

"Do you blame her?" Nathan asked.

"What're you talking about, her previous marriage?" Peter asked.

Nathan nodded. "I don't think I've ever felt so sorry for anyone as I did for Danni when Lloyd Everard left her." Nathan got up, crossed the room to the stove and opened the oven door. "He couldn't even say it face-to-face," Nathan continued as he pulled a tray of breakfast rolls from the oven. "The coward wrote a letter . . . said he couldn't stay married to a barren woman."

Peter couldn't believe what he was hearing. Danni had kept her trials to herself, and he didn't know whether it was because she didn't trust him or whether she thought she was just being considerate by not foisting her burdens on him. Peter desperately wanted Nathan to go on. "Uh-huh," he agreed, as if he knew what Nathan was talking about.

"I couldn't believe it when Lloyd walked out. Danni hadn't been out of the hospital three weeks," Nathan said while he transferred the hot rolls to a large plate. "It's hard to imagine what she must have gone through, losing her baby, then being told she'd never be able to have another, then losing her husband." He brought the rolls to the table and went back to the cabinet for two small plates.

"At least she has Kristy," Peter said.

"For how long, though?" Nathan said, returning to the table.

Peter concentrated on putting a roll on his plate. "Yeah . . . for how long?" he said knowingly. "What do you think will happen?"

Nathan shrugged. "I never did know Beverly very well, just what Danni would tell me about her. She was always in some kind of pickle . . . great character for a novel," he said thoughtfully. "She never was too good at facing up to responsibility. I was surprised when she agreed to carry her baby and let Danielle adopt it. In Beverly's place, at sixteen, I think I would have opted for an abortion."

"You haven't answered my question," Peter said quietly.

"What do *I* think will happen with Beverly's custody suit?" Nathan shrugged. "Danni tells me her lawyer says she's got nothing to worry about. If that's so, I say let her cousin spend her new husband's money if she wants to. I don't think any court in the land would award custody to Beverly, do you?"

"I don't see how they could," Peter said. "But who can tell about anything these days."

6

Beverly's bold scrawl stared up at Danielle from the long white envelope she held. The letter had come in the previous day's mail, and Danielle had read it at least a dozen times since then. Her cousin's timing had been perfect, she thought ruefully. Of course, Beverly couldn't have known that Danielle would discover Humphry's deception on the very day the letter would arrive, but it was something Beverly might have planned if she'd known.

Danielle removed the letter once more and unfolded it. She couldn't understand why she kept torturing herself. Ernest Tadlock, her lawyer, had said that Beverly had probably been advised not to contact Danielle personally. According to Ernie, the letter was most likely sent without Beverly's lawyer's approval and was further proof of Beverly's unstable nature.

Still, the temptation to read it again persisted. Perhaps another reading would give her an insight into Beverly's motives. Maybe there was something more to the letter than met the eye.

Danielle,

I don't understand why you refuse to deal with this matter out of court. I thought surely that when I filed suit you'd change your mind about talking to me.

I'm sure you know that your mother and mine, being sisters, talk often about what is happening in their children's lives. Not knowing firsthand, I must interpret the news my own mother gets from yours.

I'm convinced that Kristy would be much better off with Gilbert and me. There are many things that concern me. One, she's left entirely too often with baby-sitters. Two, she has no father in her life. Three, you are engaged in a man's work and dress the part. This is not a good influence on a young girl, and I'm sure many will agree with me on this point.

Gilbert and I can give Kristy a good home, constant parental supervision and a better example to follow.

Please reconsider before it's too late and all of us are forced to face an ugly courtroom battle that Gilbert and I will surely win.

Beverly

Danielle felt the same futility and frustration with every reading. The only bright spot in the situation was the fact that Ernie Tadlock had assured her that Beverly didn't stand a chance of winning her case. In his opinion the letter was a desperate attempt to frighten Danielle into relinquishing custody out of court. He was certain that Beverly knew positively that her victory was unlikely at best.

Ernie had been able to put her mind at ease some-what. Kristy was further able to brighten her dreary mood just by being Kristy. The fact that Peter was coming to visit that afternoon also helped to raise her spirits.

An hour before, Kristy had insisted that she get to wear her new bright-blue corduroy trousers and matching sweater, and Danielle was happy to oblige her. The color made Kristy's already vibrant eyes look even bluer. It wasn't until Kristy was dressed that Danielle realized that Kristy didn't own one single dress. Her chest of drawers was full of clothes, but there wasn't a skirt among the lot. Their conversation was still fresh in her mind. . . .

"How would you like Mommy to buy you a new dress?" Danielle had asked as she'd brushed Kristy's hair into a ponytail.

"What for?" Kristy asked.

"For wearing to places . . . Grandma's house, may-be."

"My legs would get cold," Kristy said.

"You could wear some warm stockings," Danielle said.

"Like Jill's . . . the ones with the holes in the knees?" she asked.

Danielle nodded. "Like Jill's," she said as she finished the ponytail.

"No, thanks," Kristy had said flatly, then walked straight out of the room.

Danielle folded the letter and put it back into the envelope, then quickly slipped it into the top drawer of her dresser when Kristy walked into the bedroom.

"Better get dressed," Kristy said, and stationed herself at the narrow opening of the drapes.

"I'll be ready before you can say *scat*," Danielle said teasingly as she slipped into her sweater, then picked up her hair brush.

"Mommy! He's here!" Kristy jumped up and down at the glass wall in Danielle's bedroom, then turned around. "Ooo, Mommy, you look nice."

"Thank you, doll." Danielle inspected her appearance in the mirror. She'd chosen a pair of lined leather pants and a dolman-sleeved cashmere cardigan of alternating rust and black diamond shapes. "Why don't you go downstairs and let Peter in?" she suggested. "I'll be down as soon as I finish with my hair."

"Is that the present Peter gave you?" Kristy asked as she crossed to the door.

Danielle looked at the beautiful leather oval. "Yes, it is."

"I like it," Kristy said. "Hurry down, okay?"

"Be right there, doll."

Danielle was already at the top of the stairway when Kristy opened the front door. She saw Kristy pause, then move onto the porch, looking all around and behind Peter.

"Where's Gimlet?" Kristy asked Peter loudly and seriously.

Peter stepped inside, removed his Stetson and waited for Kristy to finish looking around the porch for the Shetland pony. When the door was closed behind them both, Peter tossed his hat into the nearest chair, knelt down and took Kristy in his arms. Danielle couldn't hear what he said to her, but when they were finished talking, Kristy gave him a hug and a kiss on the cheek.

When Peter picked her daughter up, held her in his arms and listened carefully to something she was saying, Danielle remembered what he'd said about marriage and children. She could feel the sting of tears again as she watched the two people below and wasn't sure why. She'd already discounted his hasty proposal the night at his home, mainly because of the romantic situation, and decided that what he'd said was far from the truth of his feelings.

She couldn't really disagree with his observation that marriage destroyed romance and that children were fine as long as the responsibility belonged to someone else.

He was entitled to his opinion, and there wasn't much she could do about it, nor did she want to. She waited until they'd gone into the kitchen before descending to the living room.

Kristy was already in the process of telling Peter the history of each piece of miniature furniture in her two-story dollhouse when Danielle entered at the opposite end of the long dual-purpose room. She took a moment to look at the man with her daughter and was amazed at how much she'd missed him in the past weeks. He wore tight-fitting indigo jeans and still had on his heavy shearling jacket over a navy and black plaid Pendleton. The masculine fresh-air fragrance of him delighted her senses as she neared the two busy people.

"I see you're going through the indoctrination," she said as Peter glanced up from his kneeling position.

"Danni." He stood immediately and pulled her into his arms. His kiss was warm and hungry, his embrace a crushing, almost desperate hold. The long encounter left Danielle trembling, breathless and a little embarrassed, since Kristy had obviously watched with an intense, childlike interest.

"I love him, too, Mommy," Kristy said seriously.

Danielle glanced at Kristy and smiled weakly.

"Hi," Peter breathed as he looked down at her. "I've missed you."

"I've missed you too," Danielle whispered. The past month and a half had seemed more like a year and a half.

Peter held her arms out to her sides and leaned back, his eyes full of admiration. "Beautiful as ever," he said, then drew her close again. "God, you feel good, Danni," he murmured into her ear as his hands roamed over her back. "Let's not ever get this busy again."

"I agree," she said quietly.

Peter stood a moment longer, looking down at her, then turned them both toward Kristy. "Kristy was just showing me some of her beautiful toys," he said. "She was telling me that her mommy made every one of them. Is that true?" he asked her.

"It's a hobby," Danielle said. "And Kristy helps me," she added.

"Here's a chest of drawers," Kristy said, carefully taking a piece from one of the bedrooms and showing it to Peter.

Peter moved forward and took the ten-inch-high maple chest from her. "This looks like an antique," he said, looking back at Danielle.

"French baroque, early eighteen hundreds," she said.

"But you made it, right?"

"It's a replica."

"This is amazing," Peter said, looking back at the dollhouse, which commanded about twenty square feet of wall space on the east side of the family-room end of the kitchen. The front of the dollhouse faced him, each room finished with narrow cedar planks exactly as it might have been if it were a full-size house. The windows and doors worked just like real ones; carpets and draperies were all in place.

The outside wall of every individual room was fitted flush with the next to form a complete front elevation. But each was hinged at one side so the separate pieces could be swung open singularly, windows, doors and all. Peter tried opening one of the windows, then turned to give Danielle a glowing smile as Kristy climbed up on the step stool Danielle had made for her.

"It's fun, isn't it?" she said to Peter.

Peter shrugged out of his coat and threw it on Danielle's rocking chair, then turned back to the house. "What's this?" he asked Kristy.

Danielle smiled to herself. The two of them had forgotten that she was even in the room. She watched for a moment and wished she could have a picture of the two of them, so busy with their toys, a fire blazing cozily in the fireplace to their left at the end of the room. She picked up Peter's heavy jacket and hung it on the coatrack by the back door.

In the kitchen end of the long room she busied herself with a tray of snacks—green grapes, pieces of cheese and a variety of crackers. She poured Kristy a glass of red grape juice, then two glasses of rosé wine for Peter and herself. When she turned back to them, they were still intent on their explorations of the dollhouse and its contents.

Silently she brought the tray and the glasses to a table near her rocker, then sat down and watched. Peter's questions about the various pieces seemed to be endless, but Kristy knew every answer. She showed him how to open drawers, find secret compartments and turn the spinning wheel. Finally Peter turned to Danielle.

"Do you realize how valuable these things are?" he asked her.

"Yes," she answered simply.

"Have you ever considered selling any of them?"

"Never."

"Why not?" he asked.

"I noticed the belt that Katz had on the night you introduced me to Calamity Queen," she said. "Did you give that to her?" When Peter nodded, she went on. "Would you take it back so you could sell it?" she asked.

"No, I wouldn't," he said thoughtfully. "I see what you mean, but—"

"Haven't I made some that don't belong to Kristy?" she asked, anticipating his next question; then she answered it. "No, I haven't."

Peter sat down on the love seat facing the dollhouse, and Danielle handed him a glass of wine. Kristy came to the table between them, ate one grape, took a sip of her juice, then went back to her toys. They watched her in silence for a while as they nibbled from the tray and sipped their wine.

Peter was such an easy person to be with, Danielle

thought, then realized again that she hardly knew him at all. This was only the fourth time she'd seen him—the fifth if she counted their brief encounter in her father's office. They'd had one date—Danielle felt a flush of excitement every time she thought about it—and here she was feeling as if she'd known him for years. She hadn't felt this peaceful in a long time; it was wonderful to have Peter back in her life. Danielle got up to get the wine bottle and refill their glasses.

"You know, we never did finish our brandy the other night," Peter said as she leaned down to pour for him. He spoke as if they'd seen each other just a few days earlier.

"You have a very good memory," she said, smiling. "That was weeks ago."

Peter took the wine bottle, set it down on the table, then caught her hand and pulled her down beside him on the love seat. "It seems like years ago," he said as he wrapped an arm around her shoulder. His eyes held a warm invitation.

Kristy came back to the table for a piece of cheese and another sip of juice. "I know something fun to do," she said. "We can go for a walk."

"It's pretty cold outside," Peter said.

Danielle glanced down at the hand that was stroking her shoulder. "I think that sounds like the perfect thing to do. A nice *cool* walk." She gave Peter an impish grin. "You can wear your new jacket if you want to Kristy," she said then.

"I'll go get it," Kristy said, and was off toward the door.

"Pretty clever, aren't we?" Peter said with an injured look.

"Just cautious."

Peter's face became serious. "Your daughter is lovely, Danielle. She's going to grow up to be just as beautiful and talented as you are."

"You're very sweet, Peter, but she is wonderful, isn't she?"

"That's because you're a wonderful mother," he said. "You've done a good job with Kristy. I hope you don't ever doubt that."

Danielle felt an inference, although she wasn't sure he'd meant one. There was concern in his voice when there should have been none. Had he doubted her abilities as a parent? she wondered as he handed her a wineglass.

"Nathan said he was planning some sort of tea party for Kristy's birthday next month," Peter said.

"He wants her to meet his niece," Danielle said. "Would you like to come to the party?"

"I would crash it if I hadn't been invited," he said, smiling. "And I think I have the perfect idea for a gift."

"Tell me."

"Not a chance."

"All ready," Kristy said as she came back into the room.

Kristy led the way out of the house, past Danielle's workshop and over the familiar path that she and her mother frequently walked. She knew the names of several of the pine trees they passed and delighted Peter with a brief history of Sandia Mountain. In a short time she was riding on Peter's shoulders, describing sights from her high vantage point that she'd never seen before.

"You're awfully quiet," Peter said after a while. "Valverde has you worried, doesn't it?"

"Quite a bit," Danielle said.

"Want to talk about it?"

Danielle shrugged. "Friday, Park discovered that Jay Humphry isn't covered by a performance bond. Humphry denies that his paperwork was falsified and says he can prove that it wasn't."

"What happens if he's not bonded?" Peter asked.

"That's the rotten part," Danielle said. "Park will probably be responsible for the dollar difference in my bid and Humphry's."

"You mean your bid was higher than Humphry's?"

"By quite a bit. That's why he won the contract in the first place. The 'something fishy' that my dad was talking about was inferior materials and workmanship."

"So Humphry was making some substitutions, was he?"

"Aluminum wiring where he could get away with it, for just one example; unlicensed labor for another. Park and his people can't possibly be everywhere at once," she said.

"Then Park Menendez is responsible for Humphry's work?" Peter asked.

"The prime contractors are always responsible for the subcontractors they hire. Park is as honest a man as they come; he was obligated to Emmitt French, the developer, to award to the lowest bidder."

"And Valverde is at a standstill again," Peter said.

"That's right. I'm not about to finish the rest of the place and have it burn down the day they open for business."

"You could always go into the doll furniture business."

"Peter . . ."

"We'll be partners. You can use half the store. Doll furniture on one side, tack on the other. They'll be coming over from Texas and Arizona just to see the place."

"You have a very weird sense of humor, Peter Weston."

"And you make beautiful miniature furniture, Danni Britton."

"Did you know it's getting dark?" Kristy said.

"It's a good thing we brought you along, Kristy," Peter said. "We might not have turned around in time otherwise."

"We always turn around when it's dinnertime," Kristy said.

"Very wise," Peter told her.

Kristy was delighted when Peter suggested that they go out to dinner. She chose Bella Vista, a local restaurant that was so large, it usually seemed to have more customers than Cedar Crest had inhabitants. A family place, the three of them fit in perfectly with the bustling activity, the frequent singing of "Happy Birthday" and the cheerful faces around them.

"I ate a lot of fried chicken, didn't I," Kristy said as she reclined sleepily in Danielle's arms on the short drive back to the house.

"It'll make you a strong girl," Danielle said.

"As strong as you?" Kristy asked.

"At least," she said.

Kristy was quiet for a minute, then said, "I'm growing up." It was her last pronouncement before drifting off to sleep.

Peter carried her inside the house and upstairs to her bedroom, then helped Danielle get the child into her nightgown. Just as Danielle pulled the covers over her, Kristy awoke and looked up at Peter. "You can live here if you want to," she said. "I'd like that." Then she turned on her side and was fast asleep again.

"You'll have to pardon her candor," Danielle said as they left the room. "I guess we're both in the habit of speaking our minds."

"You don't have to apologize for that, Danni."

"I don't think I was apologizing," she said as they walked down the stairs together.

"Were you embarrassed by what Kristy said?" Peter asked.

"It's hard to tell exactly what I felt. My first reaction was that you'd think I'd coached her to say something like that." Danielle led the way into the kitchen. "Maybe I was embarrassed."

Peter caught her arm. "Did you coach her?" he asked with a twinkle in his eye.

"Of course not. I know how you feel about such

things . . . and I think we're of the same mind," Danielle said.

"Most of the time I have no idea what you're thinking, Danni." Strangely the light in his eye was gone.

Danielle smiled a little half smile. "That makes two of us," she said.

Peter let her go and watched as she crossed the room and began tidying up after their earlier snack. Nothing had gone as he would have liked it to, not from the night of their very first meeting until now. Circumstances that neither of them could control had separated them and kept them apart. Twice she'd vaguely referred to his view of marriage, and each time she implied that he objected to it.

Trying to remember what he'd said or done to suggest such a thing had plagued his mind during the weeks of their separation. Tonight, again, she'd brought his quandary into sharp focus, and he had to admit that she might have been exactly right—up to the point in time when they'd met. He moved to the kitchen counter to help her, still wondering about her insights.

It was true that, until about six weeks earlier, he'd been steadfastly confirmed in his bachelorhood. It wasn't only because of his parent's breakup that he'd stayed alone, although that was surely part of it. It was paradoxical, he thought, that his father had left because he didn't want the burden of children: Lloyd Everard had left Danielle for exactly the opposite reason.

"Coffee, Peter?" Danielle asked.

"Sounds good," he answered. "May I help?"

"I think I can handle it," Danielle said with a smile.

"I'll go put Kristy's toys away then," he said.

That was it, he thought as he moved to the other end of the room. Danielle could handle anything—which brought him back to the reasons he'd remained a bachelor. He'd thought himself to be in love on occasion, but there seemed to be a cycle of events that had recurred in his relationships. It was difficult to think about—painful, in fact.

As long as he was riding high, winning the big purses, staying on top of the heap, his women friends seemed happy and content. When he thought back, he realized that he'd said good-bye to the same number of women as he'd had broken bones—and he'd broken practically every bone in his body. He couldn't really blame the women he'd dated on the rodeo circuit; long hospital stays and seemingly endless weeks in a cast were not anyone's idea of a romantic situation. With sudden insight he had his answers to Danielle's mistaken ideas of his opinions on marriage and family.

First of all, at dinner those many nights ago, he'd told her that romance seemed to die within marriage. His belief had been deeply rooted, not only in his parent's trauma, but also in the fact that when he was in a very unromantic cast from toes to hip or from wrist to shoulder, his lady friends would lose their interest and drift away. There had been no commitment to stay during the rough times, and he equated rough times with marriage. What would Danielle have done under similar circumstances? he wondered as he absently straightened the contents of the dollhouse.

And finally, referring to the children attending his camp, he'd said: "The kids don't stay long enough to be any trouble." His exact words came back to him with such clarity, it was as if he'd just spoken them. What else could Danielle have thought after such a statement? She would have been almost forced to believe that he didn't mind having kids around as long as they were someone else's responsibility.

Since meeting her, had he really changed his opinion so quickly? Had simply meeting Danielle Britton turned his thinking upside down? He'd said things to her that would indicate that he still opposed marriage and children. Had those statements merely been some inadvertently saved leftovers from his skeptical past, or was he still struggling to decide how he really felt?

"Kristy and I made cookies this morning. Would you like some?" Danielle asked from across the room.

"Real homemade cookies?" Peter asked.

"Let me put it this way," Danielle said, walking toward him with a large rectangular tray, "you'd never be able to mistake them for the kind you'd buy in a store."

Peter looked down, his face breaking into a merry grin. What started as a breathy chuckle became contagious laughter. Each cookie had been shaped, as nearly as possible by young hands, to resemble a horse—Gimlet. Among the proliferation of tiny fingerprints the letter G, done in little silver candies, had been pressed into the belly of each pony. Peter took the tray from her and sank down on the steps in front of the dollhouse.

"Look here," he said between gasps for breath.

"And here," Danielle said, pointing too.

There were two-inch legs on one-inch ponies, ponies with tails that stood straight up, ponies with square tummies. Peter felt the warmth of a tear on his cheek and took a deep breath. Nothing could have brought more blessed relief from his serious musings than this gift of laughter.

"I think we have a budding chef on our hands," he said, still chuckling softly. Not until the words were out of his mouth did he realize that he'd used the pronoun *we*.

His slip didn't go unnoticed by Danielle either, but rather than be puzzled by it, she suddenly felt a warm belonging. No matter what their future held, she was truly in love with Peter Weston. She gave him a whisper of a kiss on the cheek as she lifted the tray from his lap. "I think you may be right," she said, then asked, "Have you decided which Gimlet you want?"

In the space of a heartbeat he'd decided many things, Peter realized as he stood up. "I've decided," he said softly, and pointed to an especially handsome fellow with five legs. What he actually wanted was all of them, not in the literal sense but metaphorically: He wanted to be a part of and enjoy everything that happened there. He wanted to join in and share the lives of these two people.

While Danielle poured their coffee, Peter stirred the fire back into flames and sat down on the love seat. Danielle turned out the kitchen lights, brought a tray to the little round table between the rocker and love seat, then sat down on the floor at Peter's feet.

Earlier, just after Kristy had been tucked in, Peter would have been happy to immediately share Danielle's bed. Now he was content to sit before the fire and share a cup of coffee and a pony-shaped cookie molded by the hands of his . . . daughter. The word flashed through his mind without the slightest resistance or hesitation.

He turned his attention quickly away from the tangled thought. Just minutes before, Danielle had told him that they were of the same mind where marriage was concerned. She couldn't know that her assumption about him was wrong, but the statement had revealed her own opinion as well as if he'd asked her the question outright. Take your time, he told himself; her change of mind is well worth waiting for.

"Has Park Menendez seen your revised bid for redoing Humphry's work?" Peter asked after a few moments of silence.

"How did you know about my revisions?" Danielle asked.

Peter shifted on the love seat. He didn't want her to know that he and Nathan had been talking about her that morning for fear she might be angered by it, but he didn't want to lie either. Quickly he decided it was perfectly logical for him and Nathan to be talking about a mutual friend. "I guess Nathan mentioned it to me this morning," he said.

"Oh. I didn't think I'd told you. Well, Park's seen what I've offered to do, but his hands are tied right now. His lawyers are busy going over Humphry's contract to see if he actually did breach it."

"They'll find out that he did, of course," Peter said.

"Yes, but they have to give him the benefit of a review. It would be too risky for Park to take a chance, then have a court find that Humphry didn't breach his contract. Park would face a slander suit and who knows what all."

"So what happens when they decide that Humphry is at fault?" Peter asked.

"They'll try to decide how the breach can be remedied."

"So, in the meantime, Menendez is back to square one, trying to get Humphry to fix his mistake while he waits for his lawyers to come up with some legal answers." He sipped at his coffee. "Sounds like we're talking about a long delay," Peter said.

"Could be a couple of weeks, could be longer," Danielle said resignedly.

"General contracting sounds like a frustrating business, Danni."

"No more so than a lot of others. I'm sure you have setbacks with your horses too."

Peter put the last bit of the five-legged cookie in his mouth, then shrugged. "You're right," he sighed. "If it isn't one thing it's another."

"Is everything all right at the ranch, Peter?" Danielle asked.

"The ranch is fine," he said noncommittally.

"Is there something else bothering you?"

"Remember that day in Boyd's office when I told you that borrowing money made me nervous?"

Danielle nodded. "I think that happens to everybody."

"Probably, but this business with the delays at Valverde has me worried. If the interest rate goes too high before Valverde settles down, I'm going to be dealing out of my league."

"You mean you won't be able to get your store?" Danielle asked.

"Let me tell you a little story," Peter said, then explained to her his cash-flow problems and what was involved in building up the ranch. "So, say the interest rate goes up three points before I sign the loan papers, which it could easily do. And say the store doesn't make a profit for the first four months. I'm in deep trouble."

"Do you have to mortgage the ranch for the cash you need?" Danielle asked.

"I don't have anything else," Peter said.

Danielle smiled. "The way things look, maybe we'll both have to find something else to do," she said.

Peter took her cup from her and put it on the table. "Let me tell you what comes immediately to mind," he said.

7

~oeeeeeeeeeeee~

Let me guess," Danielle said playfully, and raised a finger to her lips as if she were thinking deeply.

Peter began pulling at the pin he'd carved for fastening her hair ornament. Released, her hair came spilling down over her shoulders and back in a cascade of silk.

"You're going to be a hairdresser," she said teasingly.

"No," Peter said, letting the soft strands fall through his fingers.

"Will you give me some clues?" she asked, the pleading in her upturned face mockingly melodramatic.

"Of course not."

Danielle turned her back to him and leaned against the small couch. He began to massage her shoulders and neck. "A masseur?" she asked.

"Way off the mark," he said, urging her to move between his knees so that he could reach her better. "I wasn't referring to a change of career, Miss Britton."

Danielle glanced back over her shoulder. "But that's what we were talking about, Mr. Weston." Two strong hands gently turned her head forward again, then continued the delightful massaging.

"That's what *you* were talking about," he whispered near her ear.

She continued to look straight ahead toward the dollhouse. "Well, if we can't agree on the subject, maybe we'd better just call the whole discussion off," she said.

"I guess you're right," he said, lifting his hands from her shoulders.

"Peter!" She twisted around and looked up at his smiling face, then gave him a pinch on his thigh. "You're an exasperating man, did you know that?"

"So I've been told."

Danielle turned so that she was on her knees, leaning back on her heels, facing him. "Who told you that?" she asked accusingly.

"My mother."

"I'm sure she was right," she said indignantly. Her hands on his thighs now, she could feel the warmth of his skin through the blue denim. Her expression softened as she looked at him. His tall, muscular frame seemed to dwarf the small sofa as he sat casually, leaning back, his long legs comfortably extended on either side of her. "Don't go away again," she said quietly, seriously.

Peter leaned forward and kissed her lightly. "I'll stay as close to you as you want me to," he said.

Danielle rubbed her palms against the hard muscles of his thighs. "You feel good," she said.

He cradled her face in his hands and gazed down at her with reverent eyes. "Do you have any idea how much I've missed you?" he asked.

"Tell me."

The room was heavy with his silence. There was nothing he could think of to compare with the longing he'd felt. He'd been a man without vital sustenance, without the ambrosia of life. Now, with the delicacy before him, he was speechless.

117

A slow smile crossed Danielle's face. "That much?" she said, gently teasing him.

"Danielle . . . you can't know. . . ." His mouth covered hers, his tongue pillaging the sweet nectar, insistently appeasing his enormous appetite for her. His long fingers tangled in her hair and held her fast as he tried to satisfy his deepest cravings.

As Danielle rose to her knees to meet the urgency of his kiss, her hands moved along the length of his thighs. Heedless of the path they were taking, her sensitive fingers reached his hard, lean hips and grazed his taut stomach.

A harsh groan issued from the deep recesses of his chest, shuddering through him with an almost violent shock. His desire for her was throbbing wildly through him, but he wanted her to be ready, to want him as much as he wanted her.

Danielle suddenly felt timid, finally aware of what she'd done. She eased the pressure of her hands, feeling awkward and not a little brazen. But Peter's arms were around her now, holding her more tightly, encouraging her to stay as she was. His lips brushed her cheek, then trailed along her jaw, pushing her hair back from her ear. His tongue teased the tender lobe and traced the intricate shape, sending a cascade of shivers through her.

The feel of him through the material of his clothing no longer satisfied her. Her fingers began to pick at the buttons of his shirt until they were all unfastened. The soft, lightweight wool was easily pushed aside, and she let her fingers comb through the thick, silky hair on his wide chest.

Breathless from the rapt attention of his tongue, she swayed toward him, nuzzling her lips against the tangled mat of toffee-colored hair, kissing him, nibbling at him. Inquisitive, her tongue found one taut nipple and circled it.

"Danielle . . ." Her name was drawn out on a long sigh.

In answer she drew the sensitive bud between her lips while her thumb brushed lightly over the other. She could feel his breathing become labored; a harsh sound escaped his throat as she pressed her body closer to him.

"Not fair," he breathed unevenly, shifting restlessly against her.

"Yes it is." She spoke softly, punctuating each word with a kiss as her mouth moved up to the rugged column of his neck. "You didn't tell me how much you missed me"—she nipped at his ear—"so you'll have to pay the price."

Peter's heart leaped as her warm mouth closed over his earlobe. His hands moved down her back, then cupped the taut muscles of her bottom, pressing her between his outspread thighs. His muscles contracted with a spasm of pleasure as her hips surged forward to meet the urgency of his body.

His warm hands pushed under her sweater, then moved from back to front. Peter fumbled with the bottom button of her cardigan, finally mastered it and moved on to the next. When he was done, he pushed gently against her shoulders so that she was kneeling before him again. He slowly spread the soft knit aside, relishing the sight of her as he unveiled the image of his dreams.

Danielle marveled at her own immodesty as his eyes devoured her, and she could feel her breasts swelling in anticipation of his touch. When it came, she trembled with delight, his hands cupping her gently, lifting her slightly. She arched toward him as his lips tasted her, his mouth wet and burning against her skin.

His hands slid down her bare back, then curled under her bottom, his fingers converging between her trembling thighs. The tugging at her breast and the gentle pressure of his fingers ignited a flame that threatened to devour her. She dug her fingers into the hard thighs that held her prisoner. "Peter . . . please . . . stop," she cried in short gasps, unable to fill her lungs.

Her plea went unanswered until she thought she could take no more. Then his teeth were nipping along her shoulder. "Now do you know how much I missed you?" he whispered.

"I'm beginning to," she breathed.

His hands on her waist, he helped her to stand and began to undo her soft leather trousers. Tender kisses followed his fingers, tracing their way down her flat stomach. With the zipper undone, he eased her out of the pants and the rest of her clothing, then held her tightly to him, his rough cheek grazing the silken skin at her hip.

He looked up. "It's your turn to help," he said.

Danielle knelt again and hesitantly began to work at the buckle of his belt. When the buckle was undone, she felt almost overcome with shyness again. Her attention focused on getting his shirt off, and when that was done she paused. Her hands went to his boots, and a moment later she had set them in front of the fire. Her eyes closed for an instant, then fluttered open.

Peter reached out and caressed her arm. "I want you," he murmured. His voice was low and husky with passion.

Danielle was trembling so, she almost couldn't manage the task. Finally it was done; she eased the indigo denim down, her hands caressing the long, muscular legs in their descent. Her eyes locked with his; she reached for the narrow navy brief he wore—then it was gone. Her hands came back to his chest.

"You're beautiful," she said softly.

"How do you know?" he said, a twinkle in his eye.

"Peter . . ."

"Your shyness is wonderful," he said. "In spite of it, you're the most passionate woman I've ever known."

Danielle looked at her hands, which were resting on the thick hair of his chest. She'd been aching to touch him, hungry to see him for weeks. She was almost angry with herself for being so timid. His body was beautiful. Her fingers traced the arrow of soft hair down his stomach, then she let her eyes follow.

"You are beautiful," she said, her hands coming to rest on his thighs as she leaned back.

Peter took her hands and she almost pulled away. Then she touched him and his world became hers. His lips descended on hers, his kiss fiery with need. He was pulling her up, guiding her toward him.

Without the least hesitation now, she fitted herself against him, her knees on either side of his lean hips. The hunger of her body melted over him, opening to receive the vital flame of his manhood, pressing herself to his large body.

Their movements were in perfect harmony but almost desperate, as if they were trying to reclaim the weeks of lonely separation. The rapid throbbing of her heart pounded in her ears and seemed to match Peter's thrusting rhythm. Helplessly she murmured his name over and over again until an urgent cry issued from her shuddering body.

A low, moaning growl accompanied her cry of ecstasy as Peter's hands tightened on her hips and pressed her hard against him. A vibrant, incandescent warmth pulsed through her, the tempo an ancient message of joyful union.

Danielle collapsed against him, and he held her tenderly, kissing her hair, stroking the smooth skin of her back. She felt as if she never wanted to move from him, the solidness of his hard body beneath her a seductive force. She no longer felt the shyness that had overcome her moments before.

"I think I know now how much you missed me," she said softly, moving slightly back so she could look at him.

Peter felt the muscles of his hips and thighs tighten as she leaned back. The power she had over him was almost mystical. His eyes closed for a moment as he tried to calm himself. "No," he said, opening his eyes. "You don't know quite yet."

With his powerful arms around her slender body, he lifted her and gently slipped a pillow from the couch under her head. As Danielle lay back on the carpeting the profusion of her long hair fell in a soft cloud around her face, and her dark blue eyes were wide with passion. She watched him, no longer afraid to look at him and admire the splendor of his body.

Kneeling, Peter gazed down at the woman who held the world for him. His fingers dangled over her legs, which stretched out on either side of him, and he traced a line over her long, firm thighs.

Danielle was amazed that such large hands could be so gentle; his light touch was causing her to stir with excitement as it moved along the line of her hips, to her waist and across it. His fingers fanned out to her sides, his thumbs meeting over her stomach. As his hands closed around her she could feel the delicious pressure of his steely fingers sinking into the roundness of her bottom.

Peter compressed his lips, his eyes closing, the pressure of his hands increasing under the tension of restraint. Already his body was aching, his hunger growing, engorging with the flame of his passion.

She saw him trembling and watched his body flare with fierce boldness. The firelight was brighter within her than on the steaming grate. She was like a doll in his big hands as he moved forward, lifting her, fitting her to the newly born beauty of his yearning.

"Danielle, I need you so much," he moaned.

"Take me, Peter . . . please . . . hurry."

His fingers twined in her hair, holding his hungry lips to hers as the force of his feverish desire split the darkness of her body with his light. They were both even hungrier than before, their hearts pounding in unison, their bodies meeting with bolder and bolder thrusts. The heat of the room coiled around them, their brows damp with the sheen of joyful exertion, until the night was shattered with a mutual cry of lavish possession.

Peter cradled her in his arms, his breathing on the ragged edge of control as he gazed down into her midnight eyes. Their smiles began slowly, their kisses tender, curving their lips into happy lines of satiety.

"Now do I know how much you missed me?" she asked playfully.

Peter smiled. "Not quite," he said.

"Oh! You're here. Thank goodness," Roberta said. "Sally's been worried sick."

"Where is she?" Danielle asked.

"In your office— Oh, what's this?"

"A present from Kristy," Danielle said, handing Roberta a plastic-wrapped cookie.

Roberta smiled. "A head on each end?" she asked playfully.

"She can run in both directions at once," Danielle said, shrugging.

"Give Kristy a great big hug for me," Roberta said.

"Sure will."

"Boy, am I glad you're here!" Sally said as soon as Danielle opened the door to her office.

"I've never been this popular," Danielle said with a smile. "What's up?"

Sally gave her a strange look. "What happened to you?"

Danielle glanced over each shoulder to see if Sally was talking to someone else. There was no one else in the room. "What do you mean, what happened to me?" Danielle asked, crossing to her desk.

"You look like the cat who ate the canary," Sally said. "Did Humphry say he'd go back to work? Did Menendez say we could go ahead? What?" Sally finished in an exasperated tone.

"I don't have the slightest idea what you're talking about, Sally," Danielle said.

Sally shrugged. "Well, whatever you're happy about, enjoy it while you can," she said seriously.

The smile that Peter had left on Danielle's face vanished. "Tell me," she said.

Sally sank into the chair in front of Danielle's desk. "The phone was ringing when Roberta walked in this morning. It was Park. The scuttlebutt is that French and the other Valverde investors are going to sue us for breach of contract for delaying the project."

"Scuttlebutt, you say?" Danielle asked, leaning forward on her elbows.

"Yes—but it was Park who said it."

Danielle rubbed her hands together. "They can try it," she said quietly, then laced her fingers and leaned back. "But they'll never get anywhere with it. I can cite any number of OSHA standards being violated at Valverde."

"What are we going to do?" Sally asked. "We need to get back to work. We've got money tied up. Progress payments are being held up. The Occupational Safety and Health Administration may keep us out of trouble, but it won't keep us out of debt."

"OSHA won't help our reputation any, either. A suit like this could bring Britton's some pretty bad publicity before all the facts are brought to light," Danielle said thoughtfully.

"Do you think it's just a threat?" Sally asked.

"I think we should treat the rumor as if it were the gospel truth, Sally."

"We're going back to work?"

"No. We're going to sit tight for right now. The time isn't right to move just yet."

"What do you mean?" Sally asked.

"Something's going to break. Humphry's going to hang himself, or French is going to come to his senses, or . . ."

"Or what?"

"Or the Building Commission will have to start making their decisions for them," Danielle said threateningly.

Sally slapped at her knee. "That's what I like to hear." She stood up to go. "Hey, how does Peter like his new addition, now that it's all finished?"

Danielle grinned. "He loves it. Says he doesn't know how he lived in that room so long without it."

"Another satisfied customer," Sally said.

"He certainly is," Danielle muttered.

"What did you say?"

Danielle straightened in her chair. "I said yes, he is."

"You've got that look on your face again," Sally said. "Is there something you're not telling me?"

"I don't think so. We've covered just about everything," Danielle said innocently.

"Except your private life," Sally said.

"Nothing new there," Danielle said.

"If I were a gambler . . . I'd say Danni Britton is in love."

"And I'd say we'd better get out to the Belmonde site and get some work done."

Sally cocked her head to one side. "You're the boss," she said, grinning.

Danielle was late getting to her parents' home. She thought that her mother, father and Kristy would be having dinner when she arrived, so she came into the house through the back door. To her surprise she found Frances in the kitchen, sitting at the kitchen table, staring blankly at a roast on a large platter. The luscious-looking piece of prime beef had had one tiny slice removed from the end.

Danielle took a quick look in the dining room. The table had been set with crystal, silver and candles. The lights were dimmed to a romantic glow, and soft music was coming from the stereo in the living room. Danielle came back to the kitchen table.

"Where's Kristy?" she asked.

Frances looked up. "She's watching television in the family room. I let her eat on a tray in there."

Danielle put her hand on top of her mother's. "Mom, I'm sorry I'm late. I didn't mean to spoil anything for you." She glanced toward the dining-room door and back. "Roberta could have gotten in touch with me at Belmonde and I could have come for Kristy."

"I know," Frances said flatly. "There was no need to call you. The three of us were going to have a little party, that's all. An early dinner, the cookies Kristy brought for dessert . . ."

Danielle leaned back and frowned. "Where's Dad?" she asked.

Frances forced a laugh. "Where else? He's still at work."

"You're really upset, aren't you?" Danielle said.

"Shouldn't I be?"

Danielle shifted in her chair. "Yes, I think you should be," she said.

"You'd think I'd be used to it by now, wouldn't you?" Frances asked. "You'd think that by now I could cope with this sort of thing." She shook her head. "But as I get older, I just seem to get angrier at him. Danielle, I'm almost to the point that I can't forgive him anymore."

"What are you trying to say, Mother? What are you thinking of doing?"

"I don't know what I'm going to do, Danni. Probably nothing. You know me: Boyd gets his way and Frances tells him that's the way she wants it too."

"You're being kind of hard on yourself, aren't you?" Danielle asked.

"I'm just being truthful." She got up and began moving about the kitchen.

"What are you doing?"

"Fixing a plate for you. You must be starved after the day you put in."

"That would be nice," Danielle said. "I'll just slip in and say hi to Kristy, okay?"

Frances nodded from the counter. "Sure. It'll be ready when you get back."

When she returned from the family room, her mother stood holding a plate, staring at the opposite wall, her back against the edge of the counter top. Danielle sat down at the table again.

"You know, Danni, I want to apologize to you," Frances said as she came forward.

"For what?"

"For a long time now I've been telling you that you need to get a man . . . look for a husband . . . find Kristy a father." She put a plate with scalloped potatoes and buttered broccoli down on the table and began carving the roast. "But you and Kristy are the happiest two people I know. I've been thinking about this all day today and I don't see how having a man around could improve your existence one iota."

Danielle shrugged. "I guess maybe the right man could," she said.

"I'm not sure there is such an animal," Frances said sarcastically, stacking three thick slices of beef on Danielle's plate. "I'll say one thing, though," she continued as she crossed to the refrigerator and opened it. "Kristy thinks Peter Weston is Superman and Luke Skywalker rolled into one."

Frances returned with a salad plate of tomatoes and cucumbers wrapped in plastic. She absently removed the transparent covering as she sat down across from Danielle, then pushed the plate toward her daughter. "Boyd's pretty impressed with him too," she said thoughtfully, then leaned with her arms on the table. "Did you know that I was in love with a rodeo cowboy once?" she asked.

"You never told me, Mother," Danielle said.

"Well, I was." Frances got a faraway look in her eye. "He was the sexiest man I'd ever seen. Tall, strong . . . handsome. All the girls were madly in love with him, but I was the one he dated."

"Sounds as if you might have been pretty serious about him," Danielle said.

"I was."

"What happened?"

"One thing and another. He was gone a lot of the time. We were both young. I guess it was inevitable that we'd find someone else. Too many separations, too many temptations. I don't know. . . ."

"Where is he now?" Danielle asked.

"Last I heard, he'd settled somewhere in Texas."

"I always wondered why you were such a rodeo fan," Danielle said, smiling.

"Now you know." Frances leaned back in her chair. "I'd like to meet Peter Weston," she said. "He's always been sort of a hero of mine. What kind of a man is he, Danielle?"

"Pretty much like Kristy describes him," Danielle said.

"Then I must meet him," she said as Kristy came into the kitchen.

"Well, hello, you three beautiful ladies," Boyd said charmingly as he came in the back door.

"Hello yourself, handsome," Frances said. "Are you hungry?"

Danielle watched her mother slip into the mask she wore for her husband. Her voice sounded happy, her smile was in place but her hands were trembling as she rose from the table to greet him. How much longer Frances could keep suppressing her true feelings Danielle didn't know, but she was sure that her mother was close to the breaking point.

"Grandma got mad today," Kristy told Danielle when they were home and sitting in front of a cozy fire.

"I think maybe Grandma is tired, Kristy," Danielle said.

"Nope," Kristy said emphatically.

"No?" Danielle asked.

"She's mad, not tired," Kristy said.

Danielle felt a rush of anxiety. If her mother was confiding her troubles with Boyd to a mere child, she was nearer to breaking than Danielle had thought. "How do you know?" Danielle asked.

Kristy put her hands on her tiny hips. "I know mad," she said simply, her voice lilting over the words.

Danielle leaned back in her chair and relaxed. Maybe it really isn't as bad as it seems, she thought as she watched Kristy get her doll, Bizzy, ready for bed. Still, it would probably be a good idea to start looking for someone who could watch Kristy during the day until she started Montessori preschool in January.

"Grandma didn't get angry with you today, did she?" Danielle asked casually.

"She never does," Kristy said without looking up.

Kristy was a good child, but she wasn't perfect by any means. Frances was probably harboring every angry word she'd ever thought about saying. Boyd thought he had a perfectly contented wife and Kristy thought that she couldn't displease her grandmother. They were all sitting on a powder keg.

The telephone rang. Kristy jumped up. "Can I answer the phone?" she asked, already hurrying toward the instrument on the kitchen counter.

"You may," Danielle said.

"It's Peter Weston," she said after talking quietly into the receiver for a few minutes.

Danielle got up and started toward her, then waited while Kristy finished her short conversation.

"He wants me to come over tomorrow. He's going to let me ride Gimlet again," Kristy said as she handed the receiver to Danielle. "Can . . . may I?" she said in her most charming voice.

"We'll see. Let me talk to him, then we'll decide," she said as she raised the phone to her ear.

"Are you missing me?" Peter asked before she could speak.

A smile broke across her face. "I'm not sure I have the energy," she said.

"Oh, really?" he teased. "It must have been a busy day for you."

"I'm blaming my busy night," she said.

"I guess you'll have to tell me about it sometime," he said. "Interesting company?"

"Just your average rodeo star."

"I can still feel you in my arms, Danielle," he whispered.

Her body flashed with warmth. "Peter . . ." She heard him sigh.

"I'm still needing you," he said.

"I feel the same way."

"Then why aren't you here with me?" he asked playfully.

"You're impossible."

"You're delicious," he countered. "When can I taste you again?"

Danielle's heart seemed to be beating outside her chest. "We'll be out in the morning," she said, more to distract her wild imagination than actually to accept the invitation he'd extended to Kristy.

"For breakfast," he said. "Is that a possibility?"

"We have breakfast pretty early," Danielle warned.

"You name the time."

"Six thirty?" She expected him to rave at her.

"That late?" he said thoughtfully, then: "Kristy was telling me that your mother rides. I was wondering if she'd like to come out also? We could make a day of it."

"Peter, I think she'd be thrilled. Just this evening she was saying that she'd like to meet you."

"Kristy told me."

Danielle realized that Kristy must have been listening to a part of her conversation with Frances earlier, and wondered how much she'd heard. Kristy wouldn't have eavesdropped on purpose, but she could have gotten an idea of her grandmother's unease. "I'll call her, Peter. She probably won't make it for breakfast, but I'm sure she'll want to come out later."

"We'll have lots of fun," he said. "I can't wait to see you, Danni. It's been almost sixteen hours."

"Seems like sixty," she whispered.

The predawn light was pearly gray when they left the house the next morning. Kristy was even more excited about riding Gimlet than she had been before. On the first occasion she'd been a little apprehensive about meeting the three-hundred-and-fifty-pound pony, but today she could barely contain her enthusiasm. She talked almost nonstop all the way to the ranch.

Peter was waiting for them on the porch and led them straight through the living room and into the kitchen. The fragrance of frying bacon and fresh coffee filled the large square room with a delectable aroma. A woman whom Danielle had never seen before beamed at them from the stove.

"Danni, Kristy, I want you to meet Aggie Dobbs."

"Hi, Danni," Aggie said. Then she wiped her hands on her apron, walked over to Kristy and picked her up. "So this is Kristy," she said, hugging the child to her ample bosom. "Pete's been tellin' us all about what a good rider you are."

"When he holds me," Kristy said with authority.

131

"I imagine you'll be riding Gimlet all by yourself pretty soon," Aggie said.

"That's what I want to do," Kristy said.

"Well, of course you do," Aggie said, kissing her on the cheek. "Do you like flapjacks?"

"I haven't had them before," Kristy said.

"I'll bet you have," Aggie said, and carried her to the stove.

"Pancakes," Kristy said.

"You can call them flapjacks, now that you're going to be a cowgirl," Aggie told her.

Kristy looked back at Danielle. "This is a flapjack," she said, pointing down at the steaming black grill on the long stove. "Mmm, it looks good," she said, turning her face back to Aggie.

"This one is only a test. We have to wait till the grill is hot enough. I hear that you know how to set the table. Want to help me?"

"I can set the table," Kristy said as Aggie lowered her to the floor.

Peter put his arm around Danielle's waist. "We'll be back in a few minutes, Aggie. I want to show Danni something."

Aggie nodded her head. She and Kristy were already hard at work.

"What is it you want to show me?" Danielle asked on their way through the living room.

"It's a surprise. You'll just have to wait until we get there."

"Uh-oh," Danielle said as they turned right down the front hallway. "I have a feeling I've been this way before."

"I have the same feeling." Peter grinned broadly.

"What have you done, Peter?"

"Just a little redecorating." He caught her arm and stopped her. "You haven't said good morning to me properly, ma'am. Where are your manners?"

Danielle gave him a teasing peck on the cheek. "At least you're calling me ma'am instead of mister on this trip down the hall," she said saucily.

His hands moved over her back, pressing her close. "It isn't nice to embarrass your host before he's served you breakfast," he threatened.

"When the host deserves it, he gets it," she teased.

"That's exactly what I've had in mind all night."

"Peter!"

"Come on, beautiful lady, before my imagination makes us both late for work."

They continued down the hall, then entered the master bedroom. The change was almost miraculous: The long north wall now opened onto the spacious glassed-in veranda with a wide, curving archway. Even in the dim light of dawn, the darkened room seemed lighter and much bigger. Already, South Mountain was beginning to take shape outside the glass expanse, and the desert land was mysterious and enchanting. There was a soft glow from a small fire in the fireplace at the other end of the room. It looked like a photo in an architectural magazine.

Danielle had already seen the finished work while Peter had been out of town, and as she looked around now she couldn't see any change from the last time she'd been in the room, on the day the project was completed.

"You've redecorated?" she asked.

"That's right."

Danielle walked to the center of the room and turned around. "Well, I've never seen a fire burning in the fireplace before. Is that it?"

"Not even close."

Danielle directed her eyes to the other end of the room.

"Now you're getting warmer," Peter said.

"Is this some kind of joke, Peter? I think you've just tricked me into your bedroom."

Peter rubbed his chin and lifted his eyebrows. "Can't deny I've wanted to do that for a long time now," he said.

"Is this a new bedspread?" she guessed.

"Nope."

"New curtains?"

"Nope."

Danielle spotted a picture in a gold frame on the dresser. For a moment she had the sinking feeling that it might be one of his old girl friends. Hopefully old, she thought as she casually moved toward it. She reached for it as nonchalantly as possible.

"That's it," Peter said. "You've found it."

Danielle looked down. Her own face was staring back up at her. She could feel the smile curling her lips as she remembered why she'd sent it. He'd requested a picture because of their long separation, probably never thinking she'd send him one. "This is your redecorating?" she asked, barely able to keep from laughing.

"Does wonders for the place, don't you think so?"

"Peter, you really are impossible," she said as she returned the photo to the dresser.

"Come here and say that," he threatened from where he was leaning against the wall.

Danielle stepped up to him and rose on her tiptoes. "You, Peter Weston, are an imposs—"

His lips on hers silenced her accusation, his hard hands at her back, keeping her on tiptoe. The kiss was rough and hungry as his body pressed against her, his flicking tongue searching out the tender recesses he needed to taste.

Danielle could feel the now familiar weakness invading the muscles of her legs, and she wrapped her arms around his neck to steady herself. Since their Sunday night together, just thinking about him made her ache with desire; she'd dreamed of this kiss last night. His leg was pushing between her thighs, causing her to burn with the delight of his precious nearness.

"I've been missing you again," he whispered next to her ear.

"Peter, no." She leaned back and looked at him. "You're not thinking of . . ."

"We don't have time," he said, and began planting hot little kisses on the side of her neck. "We both have to go to work," he reminded her between gentle nibbles. Secretly he was working on the buttons of her blue work shirt.

But not so secretly as he thought. Danielle caught his hand and gave him an accusatory look. "Peter, we really do have to go to work."

He smiled. "And Aggie will have our breakfast ready in a few minutes," he said. The hand she hadn't restrained resumed the task of unbuttoning.

She caught the other. "Peter—"

But it was too late. He'd accomplished what he'd wanted to, her shirt had been tugged apart and he was kissing the tender skin above her breasts. The brief cotton bra she wore gave him no trouble; he simply pushed the soft material down, his fingers sliding under the rounded curves of her bosom to free them for his roaming lips to find.

Danielle grabbed at the muscles of his arms and tried to push him away, but he refused to be separated from his delicious discovery. As his hot mouth insistently pulled at her and she quit fighting him, her hands slid to his back, holding him to her throbbing breast.

Without her realizing it, Peter was turning her around. Her back was against the wall now, and she could feel a flare of heat as his body molded itself to her own. She moved against him, her hips straining to get closer even as she reminded him of the impossibility of his intentions.

With a low groan Peter lifted his mouth from her breast, gazed lovingly at her for a moment before adjusting her clothing, then clutched her tightly to him. "Danielle . . . Danielle," he sighed, his body trembling.

"I didn't intend . . ." He took a deep breath. "You're like a drug to me. You're magic."

Danielle kissed him softly on the mouth, then let her lips trail across his cheek. "We don't have time for magic," she whispered. "You said so yourself."

A smile crossed his face. "When am I going to learn to keep my mouth shut?" he said in an exasperated tone.

"Are you sure you want to?"

"I haven't been sure of anything since I met you," he said. "Except this. . . ."

Danielle thrilled to the light touch of his lips on hers. While in his arms the troubles of her world seemed to be unimportant—difficulties that could be put aside for a time, problems that could be dealt with at a later date. Nothing, no one, had ever had such an effect on her before. For moment after moment, when she was with him, she could forget her many worries.

Was the addictive euphoria she experienced a danger-ous distraction that could divert her attention in a detri-mental way? she wondered as they walked, arm in arm, back to the kitchen. Or was it a much-needed diversion? It was definitely a welcome and much enjoyed departure from her accustomed existence, she decided. Peter Wes-ton was also magic.

8

·◦◦◦◦◦◦◦◦◦◦◦·

Danielle saw her mother's car coming toward her on the ranch road. She honked and pulled off the road and Frances did the same on the other side. Danielle got out of the truck and crossed to her.

"You're early," Danielle said, leaning on the window frame.

"You mean I'm too early?" Frances asked worriedly.

"No, no, you were invited for breakfast if you could make it. I just thought you'd be later. Kristy and Peter will be ready anytime you get there."

"This was really nice of Mr. Weston," Frances said. "I can't remember when I've been so excited about anything."

"If you hurry, you might get the last pancake."

"I'll do that," Frances said. "Take care, Danni."

Danielle got back into the truck marked Britton General Contracting and watched her mother's car pull back onto the road. She sat there looking in her rearview mirror until the white Mercedes was only a speck on the horizon. Her mother hadn't looked so radiant for a long time. Most mornings Frances would greet Kristy at the door in her housecoat and slippers, looking tired and usually frowning. Today, at about the same time of morning, she was glowing and apparently happy.

As she pulled the truck out on the road Danielle crossed her fingers for an instant. She'd been worried all night, ever since Frances had admitted her unhappiness. "I hope you have a good time today, Mother," she said aloud.

Aggie was already dusting in the living room. Peter and Kristy were on the floor in front of the couch, Peter on his hands and knees, Kristy riding high on his back.

"I'll get the door, Pete. It's probably one of the boys," Aggie said, tossing her cloth onto the next table to be dusted.

"Thanks, Aggie."

Kristy was screeching with laughter when Frances stepped through the archway into the living room. As Peter raised his head he saw Aggie's feet. But the feet beside Aggie's were not wearing dusty cowboy boots. He looked up and grinned sheepishly.

Cocking his head to one side, he mumbled, "Umm . . . ah . . . Kristy. Umm . . . hello, Mrs. Britton."

"Come here, doll," Aggie said as she lifted Kristy off his back.

Peter sat up. Frances was already standing before him with her hand outstretched. He took it and smiled up from his kneeling position.

"This is Kristy's grandmother," Aggie said to Peter.

"Glad to meet you, ma'am," he said. As soon as Frances had released his hand, Peter lurched to his feet. "Have a seat. Can I get you some coffee?" he asked, wondering if it had been such a good idea to invite this stately lady to his ranch for a horseback ride.

"I'd love some coffee," Frances said. "Just point me to the kitchen. I'll get it."

Peter tried to keep the surprised look off his face. He'd expected almost anything but this straight-forward, feeling-right-at-home kind of behavior from Mrs. Boyd Britton. "All right," he said enthusiastically. "I could use another cup myself." Actually, when he thought about it, he hadn't known what to expect from Danielle's mother. His invitation had been a spur-of-the-moment inspiration instead of a well-thought-out plan.

"What a perfectly wonderful kitchen," Frances said as she looked around at the bright white walls and colorful Spanish-tile counters. She spotted the coffee pot on the stove and headed for it, while Peter lifted two mugs off a wrought-iron tree on the eating bar in the center of the kitchen.

When Frances had poured their coffee and returned the pot to the stove, she sat down across from him. "Mr. Weston, this is really quite a treat for me. We keep two horses at the Trujillo Stables, but I seldom get out there to ride anymore."

"Kristy keeps you pretty busy, I guess," Peter said.

"It isn't that, exactly. . . . I just don't like to ride alone, and Boyd always seems to be busy when I'm free."

Peter didn't miss the note of sadness in her voice. As he mentally took note of it he also became aware of the partially disguised discontent in her bearing and her expression. "You'll get to ride as much as you want today, I promise," he said. "Calamity Queen should suit you; she's a fine quarter horse. Danielle told me you were a very good rider."

Frances nodded. "It's something I enjoy," she said.

"You ride western, don't you?" Peter asked, concerned. There wasn't an English saddle in good condition on the place at the moment.

"I prefer it," Frances said.

"Then you'll be right at home," Peter said, relieved.

"I already feel right at home, Mr. Weston. You're a very gracious host."

"Call me Peter, all right?"

"If you'll call me Frances."

"It's a deal."

It was soon obvious to all who watched that Frances Britton was indeed an extraordinary horsewoman. Calamity Queen took an immediate liking to her, and the two were fast friends by the time Frances had the spirited mare saddled.

Art Dobbs seemed a bit nervous at first and offered his assistance, but Frances soon put him at his ease. Instead of sending one of the trainers with Frances on her first trail excursion, Art volunteered his own services.

"Exceptional woman, that Mrs. Britton," Art said quietly to Peter before he and Frances left the stables. "Pretty as her daughter."

"Agreed," Peter said.

"I'm glad you invited her out here," Art said.

"Don't go gettin' doe-eyed, Art," Peter warned.

"Fool!" Art hissed as he walked away.

But when Art and Frances came back around lunchtime, they were obviously enjoying one another's company. Peter and Aggie served lunch, and the foursome ate heartily at the bar in the ranch-house kitchen.

"So, how did Kristy do with her pony this morning?" Frances asked.

"I'd say she's going to be another great rider," Peter said. "She's really enthusiastic about it."

"Sound asleep since eleven," Aggie said. "And eat! I didn't know a young one could pack it away like she can."

"My sister exaggerates," Art said.

"Hush up, you old geezer," Aggie said playfully.

"Old!" Art exclaimed. "I'll never get old."

Frances leaned forward, interested. "And how will you manage that, Art?" she asked, a smile of disbelief on her face.

"Simple. I love my work. Keeps you young forever," he said knowingly.

Frances pressed her lips together, then smiled and sighed. "I was sure you were going to recite the latest diet and exercise fad."

"It doesn't have to be that complicated, Fran. You just have to be lucky or determined enough to find work that makes you happy. Everything else just falls into place."

"An interesting philosophy," Frances said, nodding. "Probably worth a try."

The conversation continued in a light vein until Art excused himself to go back to work. Frances seemed in much better spirits than she had been that morning, Peter decided. He no longer detected the pensiveness that had been apparent earlier. Before Kristy woke up from her nap, Frances insisted that Peter tell her about Wild Weston's Rancheros.

"But what made you decide to teach children about horses? Seems like you have your hands full just with the stables," Frances said when he was finished.

"I'm not sure exactly," Peter said. "I guess I saw too many youngsters get hurt trying to take on the rodeo before they were ready. Many's the time I wished for a good teacher."

"Then you teach all kinds of riding?" Frances asked.

"Whatever the kids want to learn, we try to teach them."

"Showing horses too?" Frances asked.

"Especially showing," Peter answered.

"Have you held a show here at the ranch?"

"I've thought about it but never had the time to do anything about it," Peter said.

"You've got the perfect place for holding a show."

"That's true," Peter said thoughtfully.

"Grandma! I'm learning to ride real good!" Kristy squealed delightedly as she came into the kitchen, accompanied by Aggie.

"Are you going to show me what you can do this afternoon, doll?" Frances asked, picking up the child and holding her on her lap. She looked quickly at Peter. "I'm sorry, we should probably let you get back to your work."

"Not at all. I planned on spending the whole day with you."

"Well . . . if you're sure."

"Absolutely sure," Peter said.

"This is grand, isn't it, doll?"

"Real grand, Grandma." Kristy immediately got the giggles. "Grand, Grandma . . . grand, grand, Grandma."

Peter stood and lifted Kristy into his arms. "Well, if you two grand people are ready, let's go find Gimlet and see if she's ready for another ride."

"I'm ready," Kristy assured him, still giggling.

"Peter, I haven't had this much fun in a long time," Frances said. "Thank you so much."

"You're welcome here at the ranch anytime, Frances. I mean that," he said seriously.

"I may just hold you to that offer, Peter Weston," Frances said as they started out of the kitchen.

Bright November sunshine filtered through the tall pines as Frances and Peter followed one of the several trails through the hills north of Weston Ranch. Kristy rode in front of Peter, clinging tightly to the saddle horn and keeping up a steady flow of questions. Being the well-trained trail pony that she was, Gimlet followed obediently behind the other two horses.

By the time they'd made the short circuit of the trail and were back on flat ground, Kristy was more than ready to ride her pony again. Peter walked alongside her, an arm about her waist to keep her steady, while Frances followed, leading Peter's horse.

Kristy took her lessons very seriously, listening carefully to everything Peter told her and obeying his instructions precisely. Peter was as proud of her as if she were his own daughter. The tiny body felt precious in his big hands, and the thought that her mother would return to pick her up later in the evening set his mind to daydreaming of a cozy family scene in front of the fire. They could make some hot chocolate and float those little marshmallows on top of it. They could—

Kristy let out a shrill scream that was even louder than the pony's frightful whinny, and Peter felt Gimlet start to rear. His arm tightened around Kristy's waist as he reached for the reins. Just ahead, a movement caught his eye and he saw the distinctive zigzag markings of the desert diamondback as the rattlesnake quickly slithered off the flat rock on which he'd been warming himself.

Everything happened so fast that Peter couldn't be sure of the sequence of events. He lifted Kristy high off the saddle, but the foot nearest him stuck in the stirrup. He had to let go of the reins to give her foot a quick push backward before the pony bolted away. He moved to save her and in seconds had freed her and set her on the ground. But the turning of his body had forced his hand through the small stirrup.

He knew, without actually seeing it happen, that Frances had dismounted and was coming toward Kristy. Then he heard Frances scream and he was being dragged forward. In the next instant he felt an enormous jolt of pain in his left shoulder. Then a very pleasant oblivion took the pain away.

"Peter."

A soft voice cut through the maze of clouds that

seemed to fill his mind. The clouds transformed themselves into tiny white marshmallows floating peacefully on top of three giant mugs of hot cocoa.

"Peter, it's Danielle."

My beautiful Danielle, he thought as he saw her holding one of the steaming mugs of chocolate. Then he felt the soft touch of her fingers on his cheek and tried to open his eyes. The first sight that met his eyes when he finally opened them was Danielle's worried look.

A quick glance around told him nothing. He seemed to be in a strange green-painted room that was completely devoid of decoration, and for some unknown reason he was lying down. An attempt to lift his head off the pillow brought a stab of pain, but not before he saw the cast on his left arm.

"Don't try to move, Peter," Danielle said, smoothing her hand across his feverish forehead.

"Kristy!" The memory of what had happened came flooding back and he tried to rise, shifting his weight to his right side, trying to get his arm beneath him for support. The pain in his chest pierced him like a rifle bullet.

Danielle put a strong hand under his left shoulder and leaned forward. "Peter, you mustn't move," she said sternly, and eased his weight back to the bed.

"But—"

"Shh. Kristy's just fine. There's nothing for you to worry about right now except lying still." Danielle placed a tender kiss on his cheek.

"Kristy's all right?" he asked, as if he hadn't heard her.

"You saved her life, Peter. She's going to be just fine, thanks to you."

"Going to be?" he asked anxiously. "What's wrong?"

"A skinned knee and a little bump on the head. That's all. The doctor's just keeping her overnight for observation."

"She's in the hospital?" he asked.

"Just for the night. The doctor assured us that she'll be going home tomorrow."

Peter tried to take a deep breath, but the pain on the left side of his chest made him wince.

"Are you going to mind me and quit moving, or do I have to call in the storm troopers?" Danielle asked.

Peter managed a weak smile. "I'll mind if you'll tell me what happened," he said.

"Always trying to make deals, aren't you?" Danielle smiled down at him. "I'll sign this picture for Penny if you'll stay," she mocked. "I'll take you home if you'll promise to come back tomorrow."

Even in his broken and battered state, Peter felt the warmth of desire as he remembered the night he'd made her promise to return to the ranch the next day. It was the first time he'd made love to her. He reached with his right hand for hers, and she held on to him tightly, reassuringly.

"Why don't you rest now," Danielle suggested.

"I want to know what happened," he said.

"You really think you're up to it? You've been drifting in and out of sleep for the last two hours."

"How do you know that?" he asked, a puzzled frown on his face.

"I've been checking on you and Kristy ever since they brought you in here," she said simply.

Peter closed his eyes and tried to relax. Every shallow breath brought a new jab of pain. He knew from past experience that several of his ribs must be broken, but he couldn't remember being happier to hear anything: Danielle had been there by his side; she'd known that he needed her. He felt himself start to drift back into sleep but wouldn't allow it. His eyes opened. "Is your mother all right?" he asked.

"You're her all-time hero," Danielle said, smiling. "She told me everything."

"I don't remember any of it," he said.

Danielle gave his hand a pat, pulled a nearby chair to the side of the bed and sat down. When she was holding his hand again, she started telling him what had happened.

"When you couldn't lift Kristy free, you pushed her foot back through the stirrup," she began. "By the time you'd put her down on the ground beside you, Gimlet was beyond holding back. She bolted, but your hand was still inside the stirrup. She dragged you about ten feet, then cut right and pulled you right into a boulder."

"She must have been pretty frightened," Peter said. "It isn't like Gimlet to hurt anyone. She's always had a kind heart."

"There were *two* rattlers. Mother saw them both."

"Where was the other one?" he asked.

"Right in front of Gimlet, at the base of the same rock that the other one was on," Danielle said.

Peter bit at his lower lip and frowned. "This is all my fault," he said. "I should have seen them. I should have been watching more carefully."

"Peter, don't say such a thing," Danielle scolded. "You know better than anyone that *any* horse can be spooked easily by a snake and practically anything else, even a pony as gentle and well trained as Gimlet."

"I should have seen them," he said flatly.

"You were paying attention to Kristy," Danielle reminded him.

"And daydreaming about you," he said softly.

"Peter, stop. Even from her high vantage point on Calamity Queen, my mother didn't see either one of those snakes until they moved. The rock and the ground they were on was perfect camouflage for them."

Peter squeezed her hand. "You're sure Kristy's all right?" he asked again.

Danielle nodded. "And if you'll just quit worrying, you're going to be all right too," she said softly.

"Because of Frances?" Peter asked, wondering what had happened after his accident.

"Mother sat Kristy in front of her and I guess she gave her a real thrill. She's still talking about racing with Gimlet back to the stables. Art and two other men drove out in the station wagon to get you; Mother called me and I met them here."

Peter tried to shift his position and couldn't. "I feel like I'm back on the rodeo circuit," he said with a grimace.

"You look like it too," Danielle said.

"What's the damage," he asked, trying to smile.

"A bump on the head, one dislocated shoulder, one broken arm and three broken ribs," she said.

"Oh, boy," he said with a groan. "That's a week at least."

"Would you believe three weeks?" Danielle asked.

"Don't put me on, Danni. It isn't nice to tease a helpless man."

"I'm not teasing. Doctor's orders. Want me to call her in here to verify it?" she asked with a smile.

"I'm not staying here three weeks," he said.

"You're not leaving until the doctor says you can."

"Says who?"

"Says me. And that's an order."

Peter tried to laugh, but his face contorted with the pain it caused. "That's cruel," he said.

"You haven't seen anything yet," she said. "I'll stand outside your door if I have to."

"I'd rather you'd stand in here." His hand began rubbing her arm. "Maybe we could—"

"You're in no condition for *that* sort of thing, Mr. Weston," Danielle said in a severe tone, trying to keep the smile off her face.

"Did the doctor tell you that too?" he asked, grinning.

"Peter . . ."

"You look beautiful, Danielle," he said softly.

"Are you trying to bribe me with compliments?" Danielle asked.

"Will it work?"

"You'd better put your energies into getting well, Mr. Weston," Danielle said.

Peter pulled her hand to his lips and gave it a gentle kiss. "At least let me think about making love to you," he murmured.

Danielle felt her cheeks flush with color. "Your doctor may ban me from your room if you keep this up," she said.

"Then I'll just have to get a new doctor." He kissed her palm, then gave her hand a squeeze. "Damn!"

"What is it?" Danielle asked, startled.

"Speaking of getting someone new, what's Art going to do about the Rancheros' camp at Thanksgiving?"

Danielle sighed with relief. "Everything's under control, Peter. Art said he could handle it and said not to worry about a thing. He'll be in to see you in the morning and will tell you in person. Will that satisfy you?"

Peter closed his eyes. "I can't miss Kristy's birthday party," he said, opening them again.

"Will you stop," Danielle pleaded. "You're beginning to be a real bug."

Peter closed his eyes again. He felt drowsy and not a little bit worried by Danielle's last statement. I've blown a relationship for every broken bone I've had, he remembered telling himself not too long ago. We've had so many problems getting together, he thought. Don't let it end right here . . . another hospital bed, another good-bye.

"I'm going to look in on Kristy now," Danielle said. "I'll be back to check on you as soon as she goes to sleep."

"Give her a hug and a kiss for me," Peter said softly.

"I'll do better than that: I'll tell her you're going to be all right."

"Tell her I'm sorry," Peter said.

"Not a chance, hero."

After spending the past few hours thoroughly enchanting the hospital pediatric staff, Kristy was tired. She'd had her dinner and was enjoying the book that Frances was reading to her. It was difficult for her to follow the story, though, Danielle noticed. Kristy could barely keep her eyes open.

"How's my doll?" Danielle asked softly as she bent to kiss Kristy's cheek.

"I'm fine, Mommy. Where's Peter?"

"He's in a room right upstairs," Danielle told her. "He's feeling much better now too."

"Can I stay upstairs with Peter tonight?" Kristy asked.

Danielle shook her head. "I'm sorry, doll. Maybe you can see him tomorrow, all right?"

"Can he come stay with me? That bed's empty." She pointed to her right.

Danielle smiled. "He's a little too old to stay in the pediatric ward, Kristy."

"He plays good," Kristy said seriously. "Like Jill does."

"I know," Danielle acknowledged. Frances had told her about the scene she'd walked into that morning in Peter's living room, and she also knew it to be true from prior experiences with the two of them.

"You two will be playing soon enough, Kristy," Frances assured her grandchild. "And you'll be riding Gimlet again before you know it."

"Gimlet's my friend," Kristy said as her eyes began to droop. "And Peter's my best friend."

"He asked me to give you this," Danielle said as she gave Kristy a hug and a kiss.

"'Night," Kristy said softly. "Go tell Peter he's my best friend, okay?"

"I will, doll."

Frances began reading again, but after less than a page Kristy was sound asleep.

Danielle motioned her mother out into the hall. "I'm going up and say good night to Peter and see if he needs anything. Can you stay until I get back?"

"Sure. Boyd left just before you came in. He's bringing you a change of clothes and a toothbrush from the house. Probably be back by the time you are."

"I won't be long," Danielle said.

"Take your time, Danni."

Danielle took the stairs instead of waiting for the elevator. A quick check with one of the nurses at the station in the hall assured her it was all right to see him again. He'd been asking them if she'd left the hospital.

She was worried about Peter; he'd acted a little strangely just before she'd left his room. For all the weeks she'd known him he'd been a warm and considerate person, and that hadn't changed. But he'd almost seemed possessive tonight, as if he feared that she might think less of him because he'd had an accident. Probably just the bump on his head, she told herself as she knocked softly on his door.

"Come in," Peter said in his deep voice.

"Feeling better?" Danielle asked as she came into the dimly lit room.

"Now I am," he said.

"Have you had dinner?" she asked.

"The food's not bad here," he said. "Better than you'd expect for a hospital."

Danielle pulled the chair alongside the bed. "Can I get you anything before I go back to Kristy's room?"

"You're staying here all night?" Peter asked.

"This is her first hospital stay. I don't want her to be frightened."

"Good idea. A hospital can be a pretty frightening place, even for grown-ups."

Danielle wanted to comfort him, to take him in her

arms the way she'd held Kristy and assure him that everything was going to be okay. But she didn't want him to think that she considered him childish in any way. His psyche seemed to be in some sort of delicate balance. For some reason guilt weighed heavily on the one side, and an undetermined and irrational fear was the counterbalance. Where was his optimism? she wondered.

Instead of sitting down, Danielle stood next to him and took his hand. "Kristy asked me to deliver a message to you."

"What is it, watch for snakes?" he asked.

"She said to tell you that you're her best friend."

"She said that? After what happened?"

"No one's blaming you for anything, Peter. None of this was anyone's fault, and especially not yours. You're being much too hard on yourself."

"Maybe," he said quietly.

"You'll feel a lot better in the morning after a good night's sleep," Danielle said.

He knew it was illogical, but he wanted to go on holding Danielle's hand forever. At one and the same time he wanted to appear strong and invincible to this woman he loved, while he also wanted to be nurtured and cared for. How would she react if she knew that he needed her so completely? he wondered.

"I don't feel the least bit sleepy," he said lightly.

Danielle smiled. "That's because you've been so lazy all afternoon," she teased.

"Always giving me trouble, aren't you? Threatening me with storm troopers, teasing me . . ."

"It's safe enough," Danielle said confidently. "You can't fight back. I'll change my tactics when you're up and around."

"I'm getting up tomorrow," he said.

"The doctor said it will be a week before you can get out of bed."

"The doctor is wrong."

"No she isn't. Peter Weston is wrong," Danielle said sternly. "I think I'd better warn her to keep a close watch on this patient. He's subversive." She leaned down and placed a gentle kiss on his lips. "I'll do that on my way out."

Peter slipped his arm over her back and held her. "You're a tough lady to deal with, Danielle Britton."

"You haven't seen anything yet, Peter Weston. You make one move to revolt against your doctor's orders and I'll be all over you."

"Promise?"

Danielle kissed him again. "Try me," she said softly, then straightened and gave his hand a reassuring pat.

There was a soft knock on the door and a nurse came into the room. "Ms. Britton, your father's back. He's waiting for you in your daughter's room."

Danielle frowned. "Thank you," she said. She put a smile back on her face as she turned to Peter. "Guess I'd better go. I'll check on you in the morning." She pointed her finger at him. "No funny stuff, Mr. Weston. I won't tolerate it."

"Yes, ma'am," Peter said, properly chastised.

Danielle hurried down the stairs. Why would her father be sending for her? she wondered. If something were wrong with Kristy, the nurse would surely have told her. She saw Boyd standing in the hall outside Kristy's room as soon as she came through the stairway door. He looked pale and anxious.

Boyd pointed toward the other side of the hall and Danielle followed him into the small waiting room. Frances was seated on the couch and immediately stood when the two entered.

"Is Kristy all right?" Danielle asked worriedly.

"She's fine," Frances said.

Boyd was frowning now. "Why didn't you tell us what Beverly was trying to do?" he asked Danielle pointedly.

Danielle shook her head; she was both surprised and

confused. Her hands tightened into fists. "I didn't want to worry you," she said quietly. "Ernie said there was nothing to worry about. I thought it would be over soon and we could all laugh about it."

"This is no laughing matter," Boyd said angrily, and Frances tried to calm him with a warning look. Boyd began to pace the small room.

"What happened?" Danielle asked.

"I went home to pick up some things for you, and Beverly was waiting for me at the front door," said Boyd. "She invited herself in and told me she'd just come by to say hello." Boyd whirled on her. "Dammit, Danielle! If you'd told me what was going on, I'd never have mentioned Kristy's accident today."

Danielle stiffened. "I did what I thought was best, Dad," she said.

"Well, Beverly's loaded for a brand new attack now," Boyd continued. "She got right down to the basics of her accusations. Kristy's with a sitter too much; Kristy's unsupervised; Kristy was injured while in the care of someone other than her parent and had to be hospitalized; Kristy has an unfit mother . . . She went on and on, Danielle, and I don't think she believes for one minute that she can lose."

"You're right, I should have told you," Danielle said.

"We've got to protect Kristy," Boyd said. "A session in court is something we have to avoid at all costs."

"Kristy doesn't know anything about this, does she?" Frances asked.

Danielle shook her head. "I haven't told anyone but Nathan, and I didn't even mean to tell him."

Frances nodded. "Nathan has a writer's curiosity and a journalist's tenacity. I've opened up to him more times than I can count," Frances said.

"No matter," Boyd replied. "Nathan's knowing can't help us or hurt us. It's Beverly we have to watch out for."

"Ernie thinks that Beverly's lawyer will eventually talk

her out of what she's trying to do. Legally she has no case," Danielle said.

"And what if he doesn't?" Boyd asked.

"I suppose we'll have to go to court," Danielle said. "I know it might be traumatic for all of us, but I think we're all strong enough to handle it—even Kristy."

"And what if he does talk her out of it?" Frances asked.

"Then Beverly will forget it and we can get back to a normal life," Danielle said.

"You don't think Beverly will be a sore loser and keep threatening you in some way?" Boyd asked.

"I don't think Beverly is vindictive, Dad," Danielle said with less conviction than she felt. "She might be a nuisance for a while, but I think she'll tire of her game after a time and get on with her own life."

Boyd frowned, then took Danielle in his arms. "I hope you're right, Danni," he said softly. "I hope you're right."

9

You look chipper this morning, Peter," Danielle said as she entered the room. "Has Art been in yet?"

"Not yet," Peter said. "How's Kristy?"

"Ready to go," she said with a smile. "Just waiting for the doctor to sign her out. She wants to come up and see you before she leaves. Is that all right?"

"Sure is," he said.

"You won't apologize to her, will you?" Danielle said, a warning tone in her voice.

Peter hesitated, then answered: "No . . . I won't."

"I think this has been a good lesson for her. She's already talking about going riding again, but she's talking about being careful too."

"I'm glad something good has come out of this."

Danielle leaned forward and took his face in her hands. "Oh, Peter. I'm so sorry you were hurt. I wish I could take your pain away." She kissed him lightly, then let her hands glide gently to the back of his neck. "Feel good?" she asked as she began an easy, circular massage.

"Your touch is always wonderful, Danni," he said softly. He loved having her near him, but his past experience told him that an injured man could be just another unwanted burden—and Danielle had plenty of burdens already. "You don't have to do that," he said.

"I'll give the orders around here, Mr. Weston," she said sternly.

"What about patients' rights?" he said in as light a tone as he could manage.

"This patient doesn't have any when I'm here. You have to do exactly what I say, or else." She kept rubbing the back of his neck.

"Or else what?"

"Or else I could turn your bedroom back into a dark dungeon," she said.

"I'd rather you just turn into it."

"There you go again. Didn't I tell you you're in no shape for such strenuous activities?" she scolded.

"Are you sure you're not the warden around here?" he asked.

Danielle gave him a gentle pinch and another kiss, then straightened. "You're on very dangerous ground, Mr. Weston." Unconsciously she let her hand rest on his thigh.

Peter glanced down at her hand. "Who's on dangerous ground, Miss Britton?" he said with a grin.

Danielle jerked her hand away.

"Put it back," he said softly, then chuckled. "You're safe."

Danielle gave his leg a gentle slap, then let her hand rest on his thigh again. "Does your doctor know what a burden you can be?" she asked, teasing. Somehow she immediately knew that she'd said something wrong. Although he seemed to fight against it, his smile faded and he looked away from her.

"Did I hurt you?" she asked, even though she knew

the light slap couldn't have harmed him. She began rubbing his thigh. "Peter, what's wrong?"

His smile was in place when he looked back at her. "Just a little pain," he said. It was the truth, but the pain wasn't physical.

"What can I do for you?" she asked, worried. "Is there any way I can make you more comfortable?"

He loved the way she played and joked with him and he wanted it to continue. His good humor returned. "You could give me a bath," he said.

Danielle gave him another gentle slap. "Incorrigible!"

"But consistent," he said.

"*Insistent* is what you mean," she countered.

"That too."

Danielle kissed him again. "Do you need anything before I leave with Kristy?" she asked.

"Can't think of a thing," he said.

Danielle took his hand and gave it a squeeze. "You'll mind what your doctor says?"

"To the letter," he promised.

"Then I'd better get going. We'll stop by on the way out." Danielle was halfway across the room when Peter stopped her.

"There is one thing," he said. "If you see your father before I get him on the phone, you might tell him to forget about the loan."

Danielle came back to the bed. "You mean you're not going into Valverde?" she asked.

"I thought about it a lot last night. With all the delays I think it's just too risky right now. Maybe something else will turn up later."

"Yes," she said quietly. "Maybe it will. I'll tell him."

Danielle walked slowly down the steps to the floor below. Usually on a commercial job like Valverde she seldom got involved with the tenants of the building she was working on. This was the first time she'd actually been close to the anxiety that accompanied the waiting when a project was delayed. She couldn't help but feel a little responsible, although she knew her hands were tied. The safety of her own people was at stake at Valverde.

Unreasonably the guilt was there. She could hope that Peter didn't blame her—she would have made the same decision no matter what her personal circumstances had been—but Peter had sounded disappointed. If it were in her power, no one she loved would ever be let down. She felt powerless, but there was nothing she could do.

Art Dobbs was in Kristy's room when Danielle entered. He and Kristy were busy drawing crayon horses on a large tablet. Pictures of Gimlet were already strewn all over the bed. Kristy was dressed and ready to go.

"We'll need a suitcase to move out of here," Frances said as she came forward. "The doctor gave us the green light just a few minutes ago."

"I'm going to take all these home with me," Kristy said. "I can show Bizzy what Mr. Dobbs taught me to do." She held up the page she'd been working on.

"That's very good, doll," Danielle told her as she looked at the many horses on the paper. There wasn't even one of them with two heads or five legs.

"How's Pete this morning?" Art asked, looking up from his own drawing.

"He seems okay, but I think he's still in a lot of pain."

"Broken ribs'll do that," Art said. "Peter's a good one for lying about how he feels, though."

"I got that impression," Danielle said.

"I've seen him walk around on a broken bone," Art said, shaking his head. "Takes a strong hand to keep him reined in."

"I noticed that," Danielle said.

"If anybody can do it, you can, Danni," Art said.

"Thanks for the vote of confidence, Art. I'll let you know if I'm successful."

"Can I see Peter now, Mommy?"

"We can go up there right now if you're ready."

Kristy almost flew into Danielle's arms. "I'm ready," she said enthusiastically.

Their stay in Peter's room was short. Kristy sat on the edge of his bed for a few minutes and carefully examined his cast. She declared that it was just as wonderful a cast as the one Jill's mother had once had, and asked if she could draw a picture on it. When yet another likeness of Gimlet had been rendered on the white plaster, Kristy, Danielle and Frances left Peter and Art alone to talk business.

"Peter seemed happy to see Kristy," Frances said. She and Danielle sat at the kitchen table, having a cup of coffee.

"He was worried about her," Danielle said.

"I can imagine he was," Frances said. "What a pity he had to get hurt."

"From what he's told me, he's been hurt a lot worse than this and come out of it all right," Danielle said.

"I think this is different," Frances said. "He might even be feeling a little guilty about it."

Danielle nodded. "He is."

"You set him straight, didn't you?"

"As best I could. He's a stubborn man, Mother."

"But a good one," Frances said softly.

"Coming from you, that's really a compliment. You told me you didn't think a good man existed."

"Did I say that?" Frances asked.

"Night before last," Danielle reminded her.

Frances sighed. "I guess you're right, I did say something like that, didn't I? But I was wrong where Peter Weston is concerned," she added quickly.

"One day of horseback riding and you have a new lease on life. Maybe you should try that more often," Danielle said.

"I intend to," Frances said seriously.

"You really mean that, don't you?"

"I told Art I'd help him with the Rancheros' camp at Thanksgiving," Frances said. "Kristy will love it and so will I."

"What does Dad have to say about it?" Danielle asked.

"I haven't told him."

"What if he says no?" Danielle asked.

"He can say whatever he wants to; I'm going to do it no matter what." Frances stood and crossed to the coffee maker on the counter. "And that's not all. I'm going to start working next week on getting a horse show going at the Weston ranch."

"You mean the real thing? Competition? The American Horse Shows Association kind of show?" Danielle asked incredulously as her mother poured more coffee.

"AHSA procedure by the two-hundred-and-forty-page rulebook. That's what I mean," Frances said proudly.

"And you'll be the manager."

"That's my plan," Frances said.

"Lots of work . . . getting judges, stewards, announcers, advertising . . ."

"It's a long list, isn't it," Frances said.

"You're going to love it," Danielle assured her.

"I know," Frances said, smiling.

For the next two and a half weeks Danielle was busier than she had been in a long time. Several new contracts and the Belmonde homes filled her days with hard work. She spent at least an hour every evening with Peter, and every evening it was harder and harder to leave him, especially on Thanksgiving, when she felt she had to be with Kristy and her parents.

Frances had asked her not to mention her plans for organizing the horse show. Danielle had objected at first. Her mother's explanation had been vague, her reasoning seemingly convoluted and inspired by something Art Dobbs had said to her about being happy. Danielle didn't quite understand, but Frances was so determined that it be a surprise that there was no way to refuse her. She seemed to think her future happiness with Boyd depended on it.

Danielle hoped that the surprise would be a pleasant one. Her mother was so excited about the work that lay ahead, it would be unfortunate if Peter had given her the wrong idea about his interest in holding such an event every year at his ranch. Still, she kept her promise and prayed that everything would work out for the best for both of them.

Another surprise was in store for Peter also. Nathan refused to have Kristy's birthday party anywhere but in Peter's hospital room. From the moment he learned that it was a private one, he'd started planning. The hospital administration gave its permission for a small and quiet celebration as long as it didn't last too long, and Nathan readily agreed. On Kristy's birthday, three days before Peter would be allowed to go home, Nathan had everything ready.

Danielle was dubious about that surprise too. As she drove to work that morning, she could only hope that the three little girls wouldn't raise too much of a ruckus. Sally was waiting for her when she arrived, a few minutes late, at the office.

"Have you heard?" Sally asked as soon as Danielle walked in.

"Heard what?"

"Humphry has just declared bankruptcy."

"You're kidding," Danielle said.

"Not about a thing like that," Sally said. "Now all you have to do is figure out how it's going to affect us."

Danielle sat down at her desk. "First of all, this means that Park Menendez is free to hire another contractor to

161

redo Humphry's work. He hasn't called by any chance, has he?"

Sally shook her head. "Not that I know of," she said.

"I hope that's good news," Danielle said. "With the investors trying to sue us for delaying the contract, Park's in sort of a bind. I know he wants us to do the work, but he may be getting a lot of pressure from the people with the money."

"You know the 'golden rule': 'Them that has the gold makes the rules,'" Sally said.

"But the prime contractor has the last word on who his subcontractors will be within the financial limits of the contract. I think we ought to give Park a little more time."

"That's what you said two and a half weeks ago," Sally reminded her.

Danielle rubbed at her temple; she had the beginnings of a headache. "I know, I know. But I trust Park to do the best he can for us. I still think things will break our way."

"Is there anything we can do to help things along?"

"If you can think of one, let me know," Danielle said.

"That damned Valverde has given us so much trouble, I feel like burning the place to the ground," Sally said.

"And put me out of a job?" Park Menendez stood just outside the room. He shrugged. "The door was open," he said. "And Roberta wasn't at her desk."

"Come on in, Park," Danielle said. "We were just talking about you."

"Kindly, I hope," he said, smiling as he took a seat.

"What brings you across town?" Danielle asked.

"Just wanted to touch base with you—make sure you're ready to go back to work if we can ever get this thing straightened out."

"Do you think we'll be doing the work?" Sally asked.

"If I have anything to say about it you will," Park said.

"But will you?" Danielle asked.

"It's hard to tell. Humphry surprised everybody this morning. Let's let the dust settle and see what happens."

"That's what *we* were just saying," Danielle said, including Sally in the decision-making.

Sally gave her a grateful look. "I guess I won't set fire to the monster just yet," Sally said.

"That's good," Park said with a laugh. "It would give my people an excuse to stop work and have a barbecue."

"You've got a crew on around the clock now, haven't you?" Danielle asked.

"And we're still behind schedule," Park said, shaking his head.

"Speaking of being behind schedule . . ." Danielle said as she stood up. "I'm sorry, Park, but we'd better get to work. I've got Kristy's birthday party this afternoon."

"Tell her happy birthday for me," Park said as he stood.

"Sure thing," Danielle said.

In the days that Peter had been in the hospital, he'd managed, without trying, to make all the nurses fall in love with him. Nathan had more help than he needed with the gifts and the cake and the punch. The procession into Peter's room looked like a parade, with Kristy, Jill and Nathan's niece, Betty, leading the way.

Peter couldn't believe what was happening when they all walked in, and Danielle was delighted to see him smiling even after he found out what Nathan had planned. Not once did she see him look the least bit perturbed or uncomfortable as the party progressed.

Nathan had seen to it that all three of the girls had several little prizes, but Kristy's gift from Peter was the surprise of the day. To Peter's relief Art had taken care of getting it there; he'd even managed to wrap the large box.

Kristy let out a scream of delight when she looked into the box, then quickly covered her mouth with her hand. A glance at the nurse in the room assured her that she hadn't disturbed anyone in the hospital, and she turned her attention back to the tiny, beautifully hand-tooled saddle from her best friend.

"Oh, Peter . . . oh, Peter" was all she could say as she ran her small hands over the leather.

"I think she likes it," Peter said to Danielle.

"I love it," Kristy said with awe in her voice.

"That was a wonderful thing for you to do, Peter," Danielle said. "When did you find the time?"

Peter motioned for her to come nearer. "On all the nights I couldn't make love to you, I worked on that to keep from going crazy," he whispered in her ear.

"Peter!" Danielle looked quickly around to see if anyone was aware of her embarrassment or might possibly have heard what he said. They hadn't; everyone was still watching Kristy. She leaned toward him. "Now you're going to see what I did—for the same reason," she whispered.

Kristy opened the last box. Inside was a ten-inch-high carving of Gimlet.

"That's beautiful," Peter said, squeezing her hand. "When did you find the time?" he asked loudly in a teasing voice.

"We should probably be going now," she said, patting his hand and acting as if she hadn't heard what he'd said. "I think Peter looks tired, don't you, Mother?"

Frances looked at him and shrugged. "Maybe a little."

"That was a dirty trick," Peter whispered as people started gathering up papers and boxes.

"I'm not finished with you yet," Danielle said. "Betty and Kristy are staying at Jill's grandmother's house tonight. I'll be back."

"Sounds threatening," Peter said.

"Let's just say you'd better watch what you say from now on."

"You mean we can't talk about—"

"Peter . . ." Danielle warned.

"—about carving wood and tooling leather," he finished innocently.

"I'll be choosing the subject of our conversation," Danielle said.

"We'll see about that," Peter challenged.

Frances drove the three girls back to her house, and Danielle followed in the truck with all the presents loaded in the back. As soon as the children were settled next door and the gifts were unloaded, Danielle took a quick shower and changed into clean clothes.

"You know what I've just been thinking about, Danni?" Frances asked when Danielle came into the kitchen to say good-bye.

"I think I can guess," Danielle said. "Something about how much better you and Dad are getting along since you started working on the horse show. Right?"

Frances smiled. "Art was right; I'm glad you noticed. But that wasn't it. . . . You won't get angry?"

"Of course not. Go ahead," Danielle said, sitting down across the table from her.

"I was just thinking that if you and Peter were to get married, half of Beverly's objections would be thrown out the window."

Danielle frowned. Her mother seemed to be serious. "Not a very good reason to get married," she said.

"He loves you."

Danielle nodded. "Yes, I think he does."

"You love him," Frances said.

Danielle sighed. "You're right about that."

"So . . . ?"

"It isn't quite that simple," Danielle said, then paused for a moment. With the other problems she had been dealing with, especially her cousin Beverly, she'd actually been avoiding thinking about her future with Peter. It wasn't easy to talk about, but this moment was as good as any other, she decided.

"You were saying?" her mother prompted.

"If Peter liked having children around, there might be a chance for us, I guess," Danielle began. "But he doesn't." She noticed a questioning look on her mother's face. "Oh, he likes children, all right, but only if they go home after a while. You know, like they do after a three-week stay at camp."

"How do you know that?" Frances asked.

"He told me," Danielle said simply.

"That's funny. I didn't get that impression at all. I was sure it was you who'd have the objections to marriage," Frances said.

"I'm still frightened of it," Danielle said truthfully.

"Does Peter know that?"

"Peter doesn't know anything about my marriage, or Kristy, or Beverly, for that matter. He just knows that I've been married before."

"Why haven't you told him?" Frances asked.

"Do you think it would make some kind of difference?" Danielle asked.

Frances shook her head, bewildered. "I don't know," she said softly.

"I'd better get going. I told Peter I'd be right back."

"Drive safely."

"I will."

As he had every evening since he'd been in the hospital, Peter looked surprised to see Danielle when she came into the room. "You're back," he said.

"I said I would be," Danielle said as she took off her jacket.

"I thought you might get busy with Kristy or something."

"I brought you another piece of birthday cake. I thought you might like it tomorrow after lunch," she said.

"Thank you," he said.

"Was the party a little too much for you?" Danielle asked as she took his hand.

"I loved it. That Nathan is really something, isn't he?"

166

"He's been doing crazy things like that for as long as I've known him."

"Well, I can only thank him for one of the crazy things he's done," Peter said.

"What's that?"

"He brought us together."

"I already thanked him for that," Danielle said. "But we still owe him one. He caused me the embarrassment of my life in front of all those friends of yours."

"Me too. But he didn't mean any harm," Peter said.

"I know. But I still wish I could think of a way to get back at him. He deserves such a surprise."

"You don't have any regrets, do you?"

"Not a single one," Danielle said.

"You looked a little worried when you came in. Something happen today you want to talk about?"

Danielle told him about Humphry's declaring bankruptcy.

Peter began shaking his head when she finished. "You have so many things to worry about. Why didn't you just go to bed and get a good night's sleep instead of coming back here?"

"Will you stop!" She decided then and there to confront him. "Peter, why are you surprised that I come here to visit you?" she asked pointedly.

Peter started to deny her accusation, then thought better of it. It was time he faced up to the facts about how he felt. "Sit down right here," he said, patting the bed. "I want to tell you something." He held her hand as he told her of his fears.

"You mean you actually thought I'd stop caring for you just because you were in the hospital?" Danielle asked incredulously when he was finished.

"It's happened before." Peter realized that she could have taken what he'd said in the wrong way. "I didn't mean any of that to sound like an insult," he said. "You know that, don't you?"

"I know this: It would take more than a few broken bones to get rid of me," Danielle said. "But I'm glad to know your secret."

"My secret?" Peter asked, puzzled.

"Your formula for scaring the ladies away," she said with a straight face.

"Danielle! What are you saying? You think I did this on purpose?" He saw the mischief in her eyes. "You just wait till they cut me out of this contraption." He lifted the arm with the cast.

"And then what will you do? Take the pieces home so you can slip them on when you need some attention?" she teased.

"You're an exasperating woman, Danielle," he said, sighing heavily. Then: "You've given me so much attention. You've brought me books to read, and cookies from Kristy, pajamas . . ."

"Which you refuse to button," she said, reaching toward him.

Her touch was so gentle; every movement of her hands excited him, as if she were making love to him. And that's exactly what she'd been doing for the past two and a half weeks—making love to him in the sweetest way possible. His realization gave him the courage to speak.

"Danielle, I love you."

She stopped what she was doing and looked at him, frowning slightly.

"Don't say anything till I'm finished, all right? I love you, but I promise, I won't ask for anything you don't want to give. I know how you feel about marriage. I don't blame you, but all I'm asking is that you give us a chance." Peter took her hand and held it tightly against his chest. "I need you, Danielle. I want to be with you . . . and Kristy too. I know it's too soon to talk about it, but someday I want a family, Danielle. Our family."

Danielle could feel the tears welling up in her eyes, and

she fought against them. All the while, she'd been thinking that Peter wasn't the marrying kind of man, that he was the kind of man who'd shy away from having children around and underfoot. Now he was telling her that he wanted a family . . . and here she was, unable to give him one. She forced a smile.

"You're in a fine shape to be talking about a family," she said lightly.

"Even the best of fathers can break an arm," he said, smiling.

"You *would* be the best of fathers, Peter," Danielle said sincerely.

"I'd try my damndest," he said.

"I know you would." She leaned forward and kissed him lightly. "I love you very much, Peter Weston."

"I couldn't ask for anything more," he said.

Danielle could feel her control slipping away. All he wanted was a family, she thought, not anything more. She sat up straight and gave his hand a squeeze. "I'd better go and get that good night's sleep you were talking about," she said. "Early day tomorrow."

Peter looked at her longingly. She knew he didn't want her to leave, but she had to.

"I love you, Danielle."

"I love you, Peter." And I always will, she added to herself. Even after you say good-bye.

10

~oooooooooooo~

We're going back to work on Valverde," Danielle stated with finality.

"I can't believe you said that, Danielle. Day before yesterday you agreed with Park that we should sit tight and wait," Sally said.

"That was Saturday. I've already talked to him this morning and worked out an agreement. Instead of continuing where Humphry left off, we'll work on the opposite end of the mall until they decide who's going to fix Humphry's mistakes. I was protesting the fire hazard, but we'll be a safe enough distance from the problem."

"This is against your ethical principles, isn't it?"

"The investors can't put any kind of a case together if we're working, Sally."

"They didn't have a case to begin with. You said so yourself," Sally reminded her.

"I also said that Britton's business could suffer from the bad publicity a court battle could bring. This way the most the investors can do is try to assess a penalty against us for the delay, and the state Occupational Safety and

Health Administration won't let that happen under these circumstances."

"What made you change your mind, Danielle?"

Danielle leaned forward on her desk. "This business is my life, Sally. I can't let any harm come to it if it's within my power to protect it. It's all I have."

Sally frowned. "You make it sound like there's nothing else in your life but your work. What about Kristy . . . and Peter?"

"The work is what keeps food on the table, Sally," Danielle said flatly. And it might even get Peter back into Valverde, she added to herself. It was the best she could do for him under the circumstances.

Sally sat up a little straighter in her chair. "I see." She paused. "When do we start?"

"Tomorrow morning. We'll work around the clock until we get caught up."

"Through Christmas?" Sally asked.

"All day, every day except Christmas and New Year's."

"I'll get right on it."

Danielle watched Sally leave the office. She'd been short with her good friend and she was sorry, but since her visit with Peter Saturday night her world seemed to have turned upside down. Peter should have been told the facts a long time ago, she realized now, and she was almost ashamed of her reasons for not telling him the truth about her past life.

Pride was the first reason. The details of the breakup of her marriage had always seemed so repugnant, so loathsome, that Danielle was sure Peter would be repelled by the ugliness of it. She wanted no one else in the world to know that the very sight of this barren woman was hideous to the man who once had said he loved her.

The second reason was fear. The fear of another rejection had also kept her silent. From their very first date, Peter had seemed such a safe companion. She'd been sure he wanted no part of marriage or children, and this had relieved her of the burden of revealing her worrisome troubles with Beverly. When it was obvious to her that she could love him, it seemed ridiculous to put the relationship in jeopardy by dredging up both the past and the present. She was positive her psyche couldn't take another rebuff.

Pure, unadulterated selfishness was the third reason for her secrecy. She'd never enjoyed any man's company as much as she enjoyed Peter's. He'd brought a special happiness into her life, a happiness like none other she'd ever felt. She'd thought her silence was guarding her against the loss of it.

Now Danielle knew that none of these reasons had been good enough to avoid the truth. Better to have been done with it straightaway than to have it come to this, she thought. It was imperative that she level with Peter, and the sooner the better. But he was still in the hospital. It wouldn't be right to tell him quite yet, she decided, not while he was still struggling with the physical pain of his accident.

Peter felt like a selfish little boy when Danielle told him that she'd be too busy to see him for the next few days. His loneliness began even before she left. He understood her obligations and praised her for taking the initiative, but as soon as she walked out of his hospital room he became despondent. He also became fearful.

Was the old pattern beginning all over again? he wondered. If it was, it had taken a lot longer this time to manifest itself, but that thought gave him no comfort at all. Danielle had brought him a copy of the latest issue of *Practical Horseman* magazine, and he tried to concentrate on an article about showing prize Thoroughbreds. It was impossible.

When the nurses allowed it, Peter's main diversion was pacing. He took to the hallways, telling himself with every step that Danielle had not walked out on him. He'd almost convinced himself, when the sight of his doctor gave him an idea. If he were to go home, at least he'd have something to occupy his mind while Danielle was busy. He was sure that he could advise and supervise without any physical damage.

She wasn't easy to convince, but he was finally able to make her believe that he'd follow her orders at home. No driving, no horseback-riding, plenty of rest—the three-week regime sounded like a prison sentence, but he accepted it gladly. Within the hour Art had come to pick him up, had filled him in on the excellent work that Frances was doing to get ready for the Christmas camp, and had let him know that Aggie was ready to supervise his recovery.

The few days that Danielle expected to be extra busy with the start-up at Valverde turned into almost three weeks. She kept in touch with Peter by telephone, but their conversations centered around Peter's health and Danielle's work. It didn't seem right to tell him that their relationship was finished over the telephone. Danielle had planned to take him back to the hospital for the removal of his cast, but yet another calamity prevented it.

Valverde caught fire.

Danielle had just come to work to supervise the eleven-to-seven shift. After spending the afternoon with Kristy putting up the Christmas tree, Sally stayed on for a while to help out, then bid Danielle a tired good-bye and left for home. Within forty-five minutes after Sally's departure, the fire was spotted by one of Danielle's carpenters who was arriving late for work. By the time the fire department arrived, a good portion of Humphry's inferior work was destroyed.

The blaze was contained in short order, but the initial inspection by the fire chief didn't reveal what had caused the fire. That decision would be left for the experts to decide after a more thorough investigation. No matter, Danielle thought: No one had been hurt and no real harm had been done to the basic structure. She didn't think of the real potential for trouble until Park Menendez arrived.

"So Sally decided to burn the place down after all," he said to Danielle after she'd explained what had happened.

"What are you talking about, Park?" Danielle asked.

"Don't you remember? The day I came to your office. Sally said that Valverde had caused so much trouble, she'd like to burn it down."

Danielle was silent for a moment. Sally's threat slowly came back to her. But it hadn't been a threat! Had it? She wondered why her mind had chosen that word. "You don't really believe that, do you, Park?"

"No," he said thoughtfully. "I really don't, but there *will* be an investigation. You trust Sally implicitly, don't you?"

"With my life," Danielle said.

"Then I wouldn't worry," Park said.

"I'm not worrying." Danielle looked Park squarely in the eye. "If they decide that the fire was arson, you'll have to tell them what you overheard, won't you?"

Park nodded. "I'm afraid so."

"I'm still not worried, Park."

"That's the spirit," he said.

The arson investigation team arrived shortly after Danielle's conversation with Park. The entire area where Humphry had worked was roped off, and everyone was forbidden to enter the site. Danielle stayed on through the next shift, pacing endlessly from one end of the vast building to the other to check on the investigators' progress. The time for taking Peter to the hospital came and passed; thankfully, Art had been free to drive him. Still, the team had no final verdict.

She knew that their lengthy stay was a good sign. A fire caused by faulty wiring was especially difficult to pinpoint. But just knowing that didn't ease her anxiety. She debated about whether to call Sally and tell her what had happened. Finally she decided not to worry her with it just yet and hoped that the arson team would have the answer by the time Sally arrived for work at three.

For the first time since the request for proposals had been sent out on the mall, Valverde did her a favor. The structure finally gave up its secret: The fire had been caused by Humphry's faulty wiring.

Danielle felt like celebrating. It would almost surely mean that Britton General Contracting would get the entire contract. Humphry was completely out of the picture, Sally was not implicated and Park Menendez had complete faith in both Danielle and her people.

"Don't get out of the car," Danielle told Sally as soon as she drove up.

"What are you doing here? Didn't you get off at seven this morning?"

"Unlock that door." Danielle pointed through the window. "We're going out to celebrate."

"What are you talking about, Danielle?" she asked as Danielle got into the car.

"I'll tell you in a few minutes." Sally started to protest. "Don't worry, Roberta got someone to replace you on this shift. Just drive, okay?"

Sally shrugged. "Where to, boss?"

"That little pub near your apartment. What is it? The Crystal?"

"Diamonds," Sally said.

"That's the place." Danielle leaned back in the seat and closed her eyes.

"Tough day . . . and night?" Sally asked.

"You're not going to believe it," Danielle said, her eyes still closed.

Sally was silent until they'd been seated in the cozy little bar and had ordered a pitcher of beer. As soon as their glasses were poured, Sally insisted that Danielle tell her why they were there. By the time the story was finished, the pitcher of beer was gone and another had been ordered.

"Nobody deserves the trouble Humphry's in more than J. P. Humphry, himself," Sally said.

"If we didn't know better now, I'd think he'd set it himself," Danielle said.

"He wasn't always such a stinker, you know," Sally said.

"I know," Danielle said. "He and my dad used to be friends."

"Until Britton won the bid for the Blue Creek condos. Right?"

Danielle nodded. "I don't think Humphry's spoken to him since."

"And he hasn't spoken to you since Roberta quit and came to work for Britton," Sally said.

"I feel kind of sorry for him," Danielle said, shaking her head. "Bankrupt. Imagine that."

"Imagine this! I could have been in jail now instead of sitting here, getting smashed." Sally held her glass and Danielle poured.

"I never suspected you for a minute," Danielle said.

"This really is a celebration," Sally said. "Do you know that it's been over two years since you and I had a beer together?"

"It's been over three years," Danielle said. "It was before Kristy was born."

"Well, I'll be," Sally said. "Where is Kristy, anyway?"

"Mother took her riding today. What time is it?"

"Five o'clock."

"Then Kristy's home with Penny. I set it all up this morning because I didn't know when things at Valverde would be straightened out."

"Good thinking," Sally said, relaxing back against the padded booth. "It's Thursday night and all's well with the world. I'm hungry. How about you?"

"Starving. I can't remember eating in the past twenty-four hours." Danielle motioned to the waiter. "The largest T-bone you have—rare," she told him.

"I'll have the same," Sally said.

"My treat," Danielle said when the waiter had finished taking their order and left the table. "You know, all the trouble we've had with Valverde is finally paying off. I think it was worth it, don't you?"

"It was worth it," Sally said, then gave Danielle a probing look. "If it didn't destroy anything else in the process."

"What do you mean?" Danielle asked.

"I mean, something has happened between you and Peter. You haven't looked happy since the morning you decided to go back to work on Valverde."

"That has nothing to do with Valverde." She hadn't meant to say it.

"I knew it," Sally said. "What went wrong?"

Danielle wasn't sure, even later, whether it was the beer or the pressure she'd been feeling that made her open up to Sally about her personal life. During the time it took to prepare their meal, Danielle told her everything.

"I say marry him," Sally said as she cut her first bite of steak. "Peter's a better man than you're giving him credit for."

"I know how good a man he is, but he wants a family and he deserves one."

"So we'll get Valverde finished on time and Peter will be happy in his new store." Sally gave Danielle a disgusted look. "Come on, you don't believe that."

"It's about all I can offer him at this point."

"Bull."

They ate in silence for a while. Danielle knew they'd both had too much to drink, but it had seemed like such a good idea at the time. She couldn't tell yet whether or not she was unhappy about talking so candidly to Sally. She knew that what she'd told her would never go any further, and the recitation had helped her to make a decision: She had to talk to Peter as soon as possible; it wasn't right to go on deceiving him.

Most of the second pitcher of beer remained on the table when Danielle and Sally left the pub. They walked unsteadily to Sally's car and got inside. Both of them sat there for a minute. Neither said a word. Finally, Sally spoke.

"I'm not driving," Sally said.

"I noticed that," Danielle said, then giggled.

"I mean, I don't think I'd better," Sally said indignantly.

"I'm sure you're right," Danielle said seriously.

"Let's walk to my place," Sally suggested. "It's just up the hill."

"Excellent idea," Danielle said as she got out of the car. "You still have the same couch?"

"Same one," Sally said as they took off walking.

"Great couch. I need some sleep."

But Danielle didn't even get a chance to sit down, much less sleep on Sally's couch. Her call to Penny changed everything, including her state of inebriation.

"You have the nicest cousin, Ms. Britton," Penny said.

Danielle's body turned cold. "What are you talking about, Penny?" she asked.

"Beverly is your cousin, isn't she?" Penny asked.

"Yes. But what about Beverly?" Danielle tried to keep the panic out of her voice.

"Beverly and her husband, Gilbert, came by about an hour ago and took Kristy into town to see *Snow White* at the movies."

"You'll stay right there until I get home, won't you, Penny?"

"Sure. Kristy might even be back by the time you get here."

Don't bet on it, Danielle thought as she hung up the phone. She quickly explained to Sally what had happened, asked for her car keys, then pressed some bills into Sally's hand for a taxi to Valverde in the morning. The run down the hill cleared her mind further, and she was on her way to Valverde in short order. Another twenty minutes and she was on the eastern slope of Sandia Mountain and pulling into her driveway.

"The Humphrys haven't come back yet, Ms. Britton. Probably stopped for ice cream or something," Penny explained when Danielle was inside the house.

Danielle wasn't sure she'd heard correctly. "You're talking about Gilbert Humphry, right?"

Penny nodded. "Nice-looking fellow?"

Danielle hadn't seen Gilbert since he was about eighteen, just before he left for college six years earlier. She handed Penny a few bills. "Thanks, Penny." She paused, then asked: "Kristy was dressed warmly enough for this weather, wasn't she?"

"Oh, sure. She wore that bright red down jacket with the hood and her white gloves," Penny said.

"That's good. You have a nice weekend."

"Sure will. Thank you."

Danielle's hands were shaking so badly, she could barely pick up the phone. When she finally had her mother on the line, she explained what had happened, then told her she suspected that Beverly had taken Kristy, probably with the intention of keeping her.

"You mean *kidnapped?*"

"That's not what Beverly would call it. But yes," Danielle said.

"I can't believe this. What will—?"

"Just listen. I want you to call the police; tell them the details—what she had on and such. Bring them up here if you have to; you have a key. I think I know where they might be. It's a hunch, but I'm going to check it out."

"Where?"

"Remember when Dad used to go hunting with J.P.

down near the Manzano Mountains State Park? They stayed in J. P.'s big cabin down there. That's where I'm going to look first."

"J. P. Humphry?" Frances asked incredulously.

"I'll explain everything later," Danielle said.

"I think I've figured it out," Frances said. "Get going, Danni."

The hour drive south on State Highway 14 took only forty minutes. Lights in the cabin windows gave Danielle hope even before she pulled into the drive. A peek into the front window told her that her hunch had been right: Kristy's bright red jacket and her doll, Bizzy, lay on a chair against the far wall. Danielle took a deep breath, then knocked.

She heard footsteps. Beverly said "Gilbert?" as she opened the door and immediately tried to shut it. Danielle pushed her way inside. When Kristy saw Danielle, she ran into her arms and began sobbing.

"It's all right, doll. Mommy's here. It's all right." Danielle held Kristy tightly to her and glared at her cousin. Beverly stared back and watched as Danielle continued calming Kristy.

"Sit down, Beverly. We have some talking to do," Danielle ordered when the child had stopped crying. Beverly sat down on the couch. "I want to know why you did this," Danielle continued as she sat down beside her.

Beverly had regained her composure. "For all the reasons I wrote in my letters . . . which you refused to answer. I wanted to get your attention. I intended to call you and let you know where we were as soon as you'd had time to worry a bit." Beverly sighed, then said: "Just look at you. Old jeans, men's work boots. Kristy's always with a sitter. She has no father, no friends."

Kristy's head snapped around toward Beverly. "Peter's my best friend," she said firmly, then leaned back in Danielle's arms. "I want to see Gimlet, Mommy. They said I couldn't see Gimlet."

"That's another thing," Beverly said. "She'd rather see a horse than one of her little friends, like Jill. Face it, Danielle, no father, no mother most of the time, sitters . . . Gilbert and I can do a lot better than that for her."

Danielle had worried about all those things at one time or another and felt guilty about them too. Beverly's argument was so logical, and what could Danielle offer the child? Material things, love. But Beverly seemed to love her too. She put Kristy down and asked her to go to the far end of the long room to play with Bizzy. Kristy obeyed her.

"Gilbert is Kristy's father, isn't he?" Danielle asked quietly.

Beverly nodded. "And he loves Kristy very much."

"Why didn't he want you to keep her?"

"He never knew," Beverly said. "He had to go back to college. I didn't want to ruin that for him. He only had a year and a half to go. The summer I was carrying her, before his senior year, he was in Europe."

"But you were only fifteen."

"I never liked the boys my age. You know that. And Gilbert had a future. His father could pull the right strings."

"Was any of this J.P.'s idea?" Danielle asked.

"He's been angry about you having his grandchild for two years, but getting you to talk to me this way was my idea." The headlights of a car flashed through the windows. "That must be Gilbert. He went to the grocery in Manzano." Beverly rose and went to the door, but no one came in right away.

Danielle closed her eyes and tried to clear her thoughts. Nothing was going like she'd planned. She'd expected to be angry and forceful and—

"Peter!" Kristy shouted happily and ran across the room.

Danielle almost leaped off the couch. The last person she expected to see here was Peter. Kristy was already in his arms when she turned around, and Gilbert was just coming in the door behind them. He had a worried look on his face and immediately began talking to Beverly in hushed tones.

Peter crossed quickly to Danielle and put his arm around her waist. "Are you all right?" he asked, and she nodded.

"Can we go home now, Peter?" Kristy asked.

Peter gave her a kiss. "Soon, doll. Very soon."

"I'm tired," Kristy said. "And Bizzy doesn't have a bed here."

"I know, doll. Just a little while longer."

Kristy put her head down on Peter's shoulder and touched his cheek with her tiny hand. "I love you, Peter," she said.

When Danielle looked at Beverly, there were tears in her eyes. Gilbert had his arm around Beverly's waist. "We've made a mistake, Danni," he said softly, then shook his head. "I'm sorry."

It was hard to believe what she'd just heard Gilbert say. "You mean . . . ?" Danielle began.

"I . . . we mean . . . Kristy couldn't be more loved than she already is. Neither one of us realized that . . . or just how traumatically her life would be upset by this. It was ridiculous to think we could improve on what she already had. It's perfectly clear now, after talking to her, then Peter, and seeing the three of you together, that Kristy would be unnecessarily hurt." Gilbert swallowed hard and a tear rolled down his cheek. "We can't live with that. . . . We've been very foolish," he said, his head turning slowly from side to side.

"And selfish," Beverly whispered, her eyes downcast.

As impossible as it might have seemed only minutes earlier, Danielle went to Beverly and gathered the stricken woman into her arms. She held her tightly until the sobs had quieted.

"Forgive me, Danni," Beverly murmured.

"Of course."

"The suit will be dropped," Gilbert said quietly.

Danielle gave her cousin a loving squeeze, then glanced up at Peter and back to Gilbert. "Do you have a phone? I'd like to call my mother."

Gilbert pointed at a table across the room.

"I'll be ready in just a minute," Danielle said, and as she turned, Beverly and Gilbert began talking softly to one another. When the call was completed, Danielle picked up Kristy's coat and her doll, then crossed the room to the door. "I hope you'll be happy, Beverly," she said sincerely as Peter came forward.

"May we visit sometime?" Beverly asked.

"We'll be at the Weston ranch," Peter said.

Danielle looked at him, puzzled, as she helped Kristy into her jacket. He was perfectly serious.

"Thank you," Beverly said.

"I'll send someone for Danielle's car tomorrow," Peter said as they walked out the door.

"I can drive it," Danielle protested.

"It's starting to snow. I want you with me," he said.

Danielle protested no farther. It felt good to be taken care of like this, and she welcomed his support.

Kristy immediately fell asleep in Danielle's lap. "My mother told you everything, didn't she?" Danielle asked as they drove through the lightly falling snow.

"She told me what Beverly had done. I already knew why." He paused. "Nathan told me the day I got back from Texas the second time." A frown crossed his face. "I sort of tricked him. It was wrong, I know, but he thought you'd told me about your past, and I went along with it. He told me everything, Danielle."

"And you still—"

"Couldn't help loving you all the more. I've never known such a strong woman, Danielle." He gave her a loving glance. "I have so much respect for everything you've done. And you've done it all by yourself, without any help."

"You helped me tonight," she said.

"I was scared to death you'd think I was interfering."

"It was nice having someone there. I needed you."

"Say that again."

"I needed you, Peter. I'll always need you."

Peter put his arm around her shoulders. "You don't know how long I've wanted to hear you say that."

Danielle was silent for a moment, then said: "What did you say to Gilbert outside?" Danielle asked.

"I told him the police were coming. They're not, by the way. . . . We also talked about loving Kristy."

"Beverly just wanted to talk to me face-to-face. I should have answered her letters. Maybe this never would have happened."

"You can't know that for sure and you can't blame yourself for any of this. You've done a great job with Kristy. I couldn't ask for a more wonderful child."

"Is that what you're asking for, Peter? Is that what you meant when you said we'd be at your ranch?"

Peter smiled. "It *was* kind of a backhanded proposal, wasn't it? I meant to do it properly, but under the circumstances—"

"I have something to tell you, Peter," Danielle interrupted.

"Then you'd better get started. We're almost home," he said grinning.

"Peter, this is serious."

"I'm listening."

Danielle felt the burning of tears. There was no good way to say what she had to. "Peter, I can't have any children," she whispered.

He looked at her. "Do you want more children?"

She shook her head. "No, but you do. You said you wanted a family."

"And you and Kristy aren't a family?" he asked.

"Not a real family," she said. "Not like having . . . It wouldn't be like . . ." She could feel the tears running down her cheeks now.

Peter pulled her closer. "It would be like having exactly the family I want," he said.

"But . . ."

"I've known about that, too, Danielle."

"Nathan?" Danielle asked.

"I'm afraid so," he said.

"I should have told you myself," she said.

"I'll forgive you if you'll say yes to my proposal."

"Another deal?" Danielle felt like smiling at last.

"The best one I've ever tried to make."

"Then I'll say yes." Her tears had vanished.

"There's more. I want you to set the date."

Danielle didn't speak for a moment. "Peter, I have an idea," she said finally.

"It better be a good one—like getting married tomorrow."

"It's a good one, all right. You know that old purple sweat suit and the yellow sneakers Nathan wears when he's writing?" Peter nodded. "What if he were kind of tricked into attending a wedding dressed like that?"

Peter's smile widened as he thought about what she'd said. "What if he were the best man at a wedding dressed like that?"

"You've got the idea," Danielle said. "I think we owe him that much after all he's done for us, don't you?" Peter nodded. "How about next weekend?" she asked.

"Perfect," Peter said. "Best deal I ever made."

Kristy never batted an eye as she was carried upstairs and put to bed. Danielle walked silently beside Peter into the master bedroom. He went straight to the fireplace, and Danielle excused herself to take a shower. When the fire was finally started and he turned around, Danielle was already standing at the bedroom window.

"That was the quickest shower on record, woman."

"I had an important date," she said, looking outside. The earth was already covered with snow, and the pine boughs hung heavily over the driveway. Danielle took a deep breath. "This is going to be a beautiful Christmas," she said.

"Our first Christmas together," Peter said, taking her in his arms.

Danielle began working with his buttons. "I need you, Peter," she said softly as she slipped his shirt off and let it fall to the floor. Her kisses started at his shoulder, then trailed down the arm that had been in the cast. "You're going to need me too," she said as she looked up. "Especially if you keep breaking things." Her hands rested on his ribs. "You're all right now?" she asked.

"Quite a bit better than all right."

"Me too," Danielle said, and left him briefly to close the drapes. For the first time she felt no shyness with him at all. "Come here, Peter," she said from beside the bed. Without hesitation she began undressing him, relishing the sight and the taste of his body as she did so. "You're a beautiful man, Peter. I love to look at you."

"Even when I'm broken to pieces?" he asked.

"Even then. You found out your little tricks with plaster casts and bandages and hospital beds wouldn't work with me, didn't you? I'm still here." Danielle smiled as he slipped the burgundy robe from her shoulder.

"I prefer this to a hospital bed, don't you?" he asked as he urged her down beside him.

"It isn't as big as yours at home," she said as they snuggled together.

"It's big enough," he said, pulling her nearer. "Just enough room for two."

Peter carefully eased his body over her. "If they're about to become one," he said.

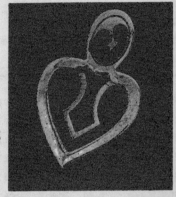

YOU'LL BE SWEPT AWAY WITH SILHOUETTE DESIRE

$1.75 each

1 ☐ James

2 ☐ Monet

3 ☐ Clay

4 ☐ Carey

5 ☐ Baker

6 ☐ Mallory

7 ☐ St. Claire

8 ☐ Dee

9 ☐ Simms

10 ☐ Smith

$1.95 each

11 ☐ James

12 ☐ Palmer

13 ☐ Wallace

14 ☐ Valley

15 ☐ Vernon

16 ☐ Major

17 ☐ Simms

18 ☐ Ross

19 ☐ James

20 ☐ Allison

21 ☐ Baker

22 ☐ Durant

23 ☐ Sunshine

24 ☐ Baxter

25 ☐ James

26 ☐ Palmer

27 ☐ Conrad

28 ☐ Lovan

29 ☐ Michelle

30 ☐ Lind

31 ☐ James

32 ☐ Clay

33 ☐ Powers

34 ☐ Milan

35 ☐ Major

36 ☐ Summers

37 ☐ James

38 ☐ Douglass

39 ☐ Monet

40 ☐ Mallory

41 ☐ St. Claire

42 ☐ Stewart

43 ☐ Simms

44 ☐ West

45 ☐ Clay

46 ☐ Chance

47 ☐ Michelle

48 ☐ Powers

49 ☐ James

50 ☐ Palmer

51 ☐ Lind

52 ☐ Morgan

53 ☐ Joyce

54 ☐ Fulford

55 ☐ James

56 ☐ Douglass

57 ☐ Michelle

58 ☐ Mallory

59 ☐ Powers

60 ☐ Dennis

61 ☐ Simms

62 ☐ Monet

63 ☐ Dee

64 ☐ Milan

65 ☐ Allison

66 ☐ Langtry

67 ☐ James

68 ☐ Browning

69 ☐ Carey

70 ☐ Victor

71 ☐ Joyce

72 ☐ Hart

73 ☐ St. Clair

74 ☐ Douglass

75 ☐ McKenna

76 ☐ Michelle

77 ☐ Lowell

78 ☐ Barber

79 ☐ Simms

80 ☐ Palmer

81 ☐ Kennedy

82 ☐ Clay

83 ☐ Chance

84 ☐ Powers

85 ☐ James

86 ☐ Malek

YOU'LL BE SWEPT AWAY WITH SILHOUETTE DESIRE

$1.95 each

87 ☐ Michelle	105 ☐ Blair	123 ☐ Paige	141 ☐ Morgan
88 ☐ Trevor	106 ☐ Michelle	124 ☐ St. George	142 ☐ Nicole
89 ☐ Ross	107 ☐ Chance	125 ☐ Caimi	143 ☐ Allison
90 ☐ Roszel	108 ☐ Gladstone	126 ☐ Carey	144 ☐ Evans
91 ☐ Browning	109 ☐ Simms	127 ☐ James	145 ☐ James
92 ☐ Carey	110 ☐ Palmer	128 ☐ Michelle	146 ☐ Knight
93 ☐ Berk	111 ☐ Browning	129 ☐ Bishop	147 ☐ Scott
94 ☐ Robbins	112 ☐ Nicole	130 ☐ Blair	148 ☐ Powers
95 ☐ Summers	113 ☐ Cresswell	131 ☐ Larson	149 ☐ Galt
96 ☐ Milan	114 ☐ Ross	132 ☐ McCoy	150 ☐ Simms
97 ☐ James	115 ☐ James	133 ☐ Monet	151 ☐ Major
98 ☐ Joyce	116 ☐ Joyce	134 ☐ McKenna	152 ☐ Michelle
99 ☐ Major	117 ☐ Powers	135 ☐ Charlton	153 ☐ Milan
100 ☐ Howard	118 ☐ Milan	136 ☐ Martel	154 ☐ Berk
101 ☐ Morgan	119 ☐ John	137 ☐ Ross	155 ☐ Ross
102 ☐ Palmer	120 ☐ Clay	138 ☐ Chase	156 ☐ Corbett
103 ☐ James	121 ☐ Browning	139 ☐ St. Claire	
104 ☐ Chase	122 ☐ Trent	140 ☐ Joyce	

SILHOUETTE DESIRE, Department SD/6
1230 Avenue of the Americas
New York, NY 10020

Please send me the books I have checked above. I am enclosing $_____
(please add 75¢ to cover postage and handling. NYS and NYC residents please
add appropriate sales tax). Send check or money order—no cash or C.O.D.'s
please. Allow six weeks for delivery.

NAME_____

ADDRESS_____

CITY_____ STATE/ZIP_____

Enjoy romance and passion, larger-than-life...

Now, thrill to 4
Silhouette Intimate Moments
novels (a $9.00 value)—
ABSOLUTELY FREE!

If you want more passionate sensual romance, then Silhouette Intimate Moments novels are for you!

In every 256-page book, you'll find romance that's electrifying...involving... and intense. And now, these larger-than-life romances can come into your home every month!

4 FREE books as your introduction.

Act now and we'll send you four thrilling Silhouette Intimate Moments novels. They're our gift to introduce you to our convenient home subscription service. Every month, we'll send you four new Silhouette Intimate Moments books. Look them over for 15 days. If you keep them, pay just $9.00 for all four. Or return them at no charge.

We'll mail your books to you *as soon as they are published.* Plus, with every shipment, you'll receive the Silhouette Books Newsletter absolutely free. *And Silhouette Intimate Moments is delivered free.*

Mail the coupon today and start receiving Silhouette Intimate Moments. Romance novels for women...not girls.

Silhouette Intimate Moments

Silhouette Intimate Moments™
120 Brighton Road, P.O. Box 5020, Clifton, NJ 07015

☐ YES! Please send me FREE and without obligation, 4 exciting Silhouette Intimate Moments romance novels. Unless you hear from me after I receive my 4 FREE books, please send 4 new Silhouette Intimate Moments novels to preview each month. I understand that you will bill me $2.25 each for a total of $9.00 — with no additional shipping, handling or other charges. **There is no minimum number of books to buy and I may cancel anytime I wish.** The first 4 books are mine to keep, even if I never take a single additional book.

☐ Mrs. ☐ Miss ☐ Ms. ☐ Mr.   **BMD824**

Name	(please print)
Address	Apt. #
City ( )	State Zip
Area Code Telephone Number	

Signature (if under 18, parent or guardian must sign)

This offer, limited to one per household, expires February 28, 1985. Terms and prices subject to change. Your enrollment is subject to acceptance by Simon & Schuster Enterprises.

Silhouette Intimate Moments is a service mark and trademark of Simon & Schuster, Inc.

Coming Next Month

The Rawhide Man by Diana Palmer

Bess had always thought of Jude as rough and hard as rawhide—then she discovered another side of him. Their marriage was one of convenience, but then Jude unexpectedly captured her heart.

Rapture Of The Deep by Barbara Cameron

Lori poured all the affection she found hard to express into her work with dolphins—until Jordan pirated her away to the high seas! How had he known she would be able to abandon herself to love there as she never could on shore?

Velvet Is For Lovers by Edith St. George

Alyson was all set to go diving for the sunken galleon—but she didn't know her greatest challenge on the expedition would be its leader, Ivan Kyriokos. Soon she found herself looking for the most important treasure of all—his love!

Moon On East Mountain by Hope McIntyre

City planner Clover McBain clashed by day with Roarke Deveraux over their excavations, but the Korean nights found them unable to resist one another's arms. Could the wisdom of the ages show them the peace that lies in loving compromise?

Through Laughter And Tears by Marie Nicole

Sam had always used humor to mask her feelings of inadequacy—but her armor failed her with talent agent Jake Benedict. He saw right through her, but she *had* to keep him from finding out that, more than his client, she wanted to be his woman.

Dream Builder by Naomi Horton

Lindsay's independence had come at a high price, but she had learned to survive without Ryan—and without love—until he suddenly walked back into her life. Dark and moody Ryan had broken her heart once; did she dare trust him with it again?